'I do not wish to have anything further to do with you,' she said in clearly enunciated tones. **'Please leave.'**

'Listen, sweetheart,' Lucca said, with a cavalier disregard for protocol. 'Way I see it, we're stuck with each other, at least for the sake of appearances. Your big sister seems pretty keen on us working together and I get the feeling that what she says around here goes. Quite frankly, I'd rather be working on my tan on one of your beaches, preferably with a couple of blonde beach bunnies peeling grapes for me. So kick me out if you dare. I'm cool with it, but you can say goodbye to using The Chatsfield.'

She turned and gave him a look one would do when a cockroach appears on the table in the middle of a formal dining setting. 'You are the most disreputable man I have ever met.'

'Looks like you need to get out more.' He gave her his fallen angel's smile. 'I can assure you there's plenty more out there like me.'

Her eyes slitted like a cat facing a feral dog, her hands balling into fists at her sides. 'Get out before I have you thrown out by my security team.'

He gave an indolent shrug as he ambled over to the door. 'I'll be staying in the penthouse at The Chatsfield if you want me.' H̲ ̲ ̲ ̲ ̲ ̲ ̲oss his open palm.

THE CHATSFIELD

Sheikh's Scandal
LUCY MONROE
May 2014

Playboy's Lesson
MELANIE MILBURNE
June 2014

Socialite's Gamble
MICHELLE CONDER
July 2014

Billionaire's Secret
CHANTELLE SHAW
August 2014

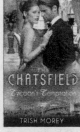

Tycoon's Temptation
TRISH MOREY
September 2014

Rival's Challenge
ABBY GREEN
October 2014

Rebel's Bargain
ANNIE WEST
November 2014

Heiress's Defiance
LYNN RAYE HARRIS
December 2014

Step into the opulent glory of the world's most elite hotel, where clients are the impossibly rich and exceptionally famous.

Whether you're in America, Australia, Europe or Dubai, our doors will always be open…

Welcome to

THE CHATSFIELD

Synonymous with style, sensation…and scandal!

For years, the children of Gene Chatsfield—global hotel entrepreneur—have shocked the world's media with their exploits. But no longer! When Gene appoints a new CEO, Christos Giatrakos, to bring his children into line, little did he know what he was starting.

Christos' first command scatters the Chatsfields to the furthest reaches of their international holdings—from Las Vegas to Monte Carlo, Sydney to San Francisco…but will they rise to the challenge set by a man who hides dark secrets in his past?

Let the games begin!

Your room has been reserved, so check in to enjoy all the passion and scandal we have to offer.

Ref: 00106875

www.thechatsfield.com

Published in Great Britain 2014
by Mills & Boon, an imprint of Harlequin (UK) Limited,
Eton House, 18-24 Paradise Road, Richmond, Surrey, TW9 1SR

© 2014 Harlequin Books S.A.

Special thanks and acknowledgement are given to Melanie Milburne for her contribution to The Chatsfield series.

ISBN: 978-0-263-24622-3

053-0614

Harlequin (UK) Limited's policy is to use papers that are natural, renewable and recyclable products and made from wood grown in sustainable forests. The logging and manufacturing processes conform to the legal environmental regulations of the country of origin.

Printed and bound in Spain
by Blackprint CPI, Barcelona

PLAYBOY'S LESSON

BY
MELANIE MILBURNE

MILLS & BOON

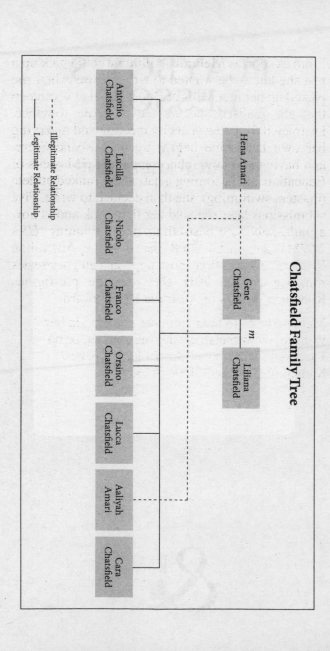

Chatsfield Family Tree

Hena Amari

Gene Chatsfield

m

Liliana Chatsfield

Antonio Chatsfield

Lucilla Chatsfield

Nicolo Chatsfield

Franco Chatsfield

Orsino Chatsfield

Lucca Chatsfield

Aaliyah Amari

Cara Chatsfield

----- Illegitimate Relationship

——— Legitimate Relationship

From as soon as **Melanie Milburne** could pick up a pen she knew she wanted to write. It was when she picked up her first Mills & Boon® novel at seventeen that she realised she wanted to write romance. Distracted for a few years by meeting and marrying her own handsome hero, surgeon husband Steve, and having two boys, plus completing a Master's of Education and becoming a nationally ranked athlete (masters swimming), she then decided to write. Five submissions later she sold her first book and is now a multi-published bestselling, award-winning, *USA TODAY* author. In 2008 she won the Australian Readers' Association most popular category/series romance and in 2011 she won the prestigious Romance Writers of Australia R*BY award.

Melanie loves to hear from her readers via her website, www.melaniemilburne.com.au, or on Facebook: http://www.facebook.com/pages/Melanie-Milburne/351594482609.

To my fellow Chatsfield authors:

Lucy Monroe, Michelle Conder,
Chantelle Shaw, Trish Morey, Abby Green,
Annie West, Lynn Raye Harris.

Wasn't this huge fun? I loved doing this
continuity with you all. xxx

CHAPTER ONE

EVEN BY CHATSFIELD standards Lucca had to admit this latest one of his to hit the London tabloids was a doozy. He lounged in the chair opposite his father's new broom, Christos Giatrakos, and gave one his trademark lazy smiles. 'What was it that got up your nose? The handcuffs or the studded leather codpiece?'

What the newly appointed CEO of the Chatsfield Hotel chain lacked in terms of a sense of humour was more than made up for in ice-cold ruthlessness. The Greek's face was set like marble, his blue eyes glacial and his mouth set in a line so thin it hinted at a streak of cruelty underpinning his intractable personality. 'We're used to reading your sordid exploits in the tabloids, but this news is all over the internet. You've brought nothing but shame to the brand of this hotel with the way you carry on your affairs.'

Yeah, yeah, yeah. Lucca didn't bother disguising a yawn. *Bor-ing.* Heard it all before. A hundred…probably trillions of times. He rocked back on the legs of the chair, expertly balancing his weight as he kept his gaze trained on the hardened CEO. He was used to showdown meetings like this. He enjoyed them. It was his way of making up for the way he had disgraced himself by wetting his pants when he was called into the headmaster's office at boarding school when he was seven. He never allowed himself to be intimidated.

Never.

'The only thing that's predictable about you is your unpredictability,' the CEO continued. 'Since you've consistently refused to clean up your act, it will now be cleaned up for you.'

'It was just a party that got a little out of hand,' Lucca said. 'The press made it out to be an orgy. I didn't even sleep with any of those girls. Well, maybe just the one, but that was because I was handcuffed to the bed at the time, so what else was I supposed to do?'

A muscle in the CEO's jaw pulsed. On. Off. 'Your father is refusing to give you a single penny of your allowance from the Chatsfield Family Trust unless you agree to fulfil the assignment I have appointed you. It will make quite a change for you working for a living instead of being a professional party boy with nothing better to do than get laid by a host of wannabe starlets and trashy gold-diggers.'

Lucca set his chair legs back down on the carpeted floor with a little thump. He had an exclusive art auction he wanted to attend in Monte Carlo next week. He was building a private collection of miniature paintings and there was one in particular he wanted to get his hands on. His gut instinct told him it would be worth millions in a few years. He didn't want to be exiled to some god-forsaken place and miss out on the deal of a lifetime, but neither did he want to forfeit his allowance.

The way he saw it, his family—his train wreck of a family—owed it to him.

'What sort of mission?'

'A month working at the Chatsfield Hotel on the island of Preitalle in the Mediterranean.'

Lucca mentally breathed out a sigh of relief. The royal principality of Preitalle was a short ferry trip or helicopter ride to Monte Carlo. But he figured it might be in his interests to appear unhappy about being exiled. His father's CEO wanted to dish out punishment and he clearly was enjoying doing it. Just like that headmaster.

Bastard.

'Doing what?' He feigned a suitable amount of apprehension. That was all part of his game. Give the opponent what they want but only on the outside. Inside he was totally in control. Totally.

The CEO's cold eyes gleamed with malice. 'Working alongside Her Royal Highness Princess Charlotte as she plans her sister Madeleine's wedding at the end of the month.'

Lucca threw his head back and laughed so loudly the sound bounced off the walls and came back at him like an echo in a canyon. 'You're joking, right? *Me?* Plan a wedding? I know nothing about wedding planning. Parties? Yes. Weddings? Zilch. Can't even remember the last time I went to one.'

'Then this will be a perfect opportunity to learn.' Christos clicked his pen on and off again as he eyeballed him. On. Off. The annoying sound was in perfect time with that muscle in his jaw. On. Off. 'You're reputedly an expert at knowing what women want. Here's your chance to finally put that expertise to good use.'

Lucca decided to play along. How hard could it be? With the wedding this close, the bulk of the planning would have already been done. He would leave the last-minute work to the people who knew how to do this sort of stuff while he had a bit of time out on one of the beaches on Preitalle.

He was getting a bit tired of the London scene in any case. It used to be so much fun, courting scandal, poking fun at the establishment, doing the most outrageous things he could think of just for the heck of it. Exploiting every situation to his advantage. But there was only so much partying and nightclubbing and sleeping around any man could do. It was exhausting.

Even—dared he say it—boring?

Besides, he wanted more time to concentrate on his art. Not just the ones he was collecting but his own etchings. His passion for drawing had been present from the moment he had been old enough to hold a pencil in his hand. Drawing was his way of retreating into a private world where he could be quiet and centred. It had been his way of anchoring himself during his chaotic childhood. The eye of the family storm could bluster and blow all around him but he could always escape to his inner world of creative peace. He had spent hours sitting cross-legged beneath Graham Laurent's painting of his mother, desperately trying to capture the features that were fast fading from his memory, yet somehow resolutely captured for all time in the portrait before him. He enjoyed the process of creating those first scratches of a pencil on a tiny canvas to the end result of having a framed miniature painting with his signature in the right-hand corner.

Spending the month of June in the Mediterranean would be just the ticket to indulge that passion instead of his more base ones. It would be easy. He would jump through the hoops and have a whoop of a time doing it.

'So—' he rocked back in his chair again '—what does the little princess think about having an offsider?'

* * *

'An offsider?' Lottie looked at her sister, Madeleine, in wounded affront. 'Why do you think I need someone to help me? Don't you think I'm up to the task of planning your wedding? Did Mama suggest it? Papa? One of the palace officials?'

Madeleine held up her hands as if warding off a barrage of enemy fire. 'Whoa, there! No need to shoot the messenger. It's part of the deal with conducting the reception at the Chatsfield Hotel. It's come from the top level of management but I've given it my full approval. The CEO is sending a representative of the Chatsfield family to work alongside you in the interest of public relations.'

'But I've already done all the planning.' Lottie rapped her knuckles on the encyclopedia-thick folder she had brought with her. 'Every minute detail is set out in there. The last thing I need right now is someone coming in to change everything at the last minute.'

Madeleine lounged back in her seat and elegantly crossed one leg over the other as she inspected her newly painted toenails. 'I think it will be good for you to have someone to share the workload with.' She looked up with an I-know-better-than-you look that always grated on Lottie's nerves like a rasp on a raw wound. 'Someone young and hip and a little more in touch with the party scene.'

Lottie narrowed her gaze as the back of her neck began to prickle. 'Who are they sending?'

'One of the twin brothers.'

She knew her sister thought her a little out of touch with the modern world but did she have to make it so obvious by recruiting someone who did nothing *but* party? The Chatsfield twins, Lucca and Orsino, were notorious bad boys who were in and out of the press almost weekly with their wild exploits.

Hells bells...please let it not be... 'Which one?'

'Lucca.'

Lottie blinked. Twice. Three times. 'Did you say...?'

Madeleine nodded. 'Yup.'

Lottie gulped. 'The one whose photograph has been splashed all over the internet? The one in that hotel room wearing nothing but a studded leather—whatever it's called?'

'Codpiece.'

She clapped a hand over her forehead. 'Oh, dear God.'

'I'm sure he'll behave himself impeccably while he's here,' Madeleine assured her. At least even the scandalous Lucca Chatsfield had drawn a line at posting a selfie of *that* picture on Twitter, Lottie thought.

'Word has it his allowance from the Chatsfield Family Trust will be cut off if he doesn't.'

Lottie dropped her hand and scowled at her sister. 'So I'm to be some sort of behaviour modification coach or something? Who on earth thought of this ridiculous scheme? Are you sure it's not a joke? Tell me it's a joke.'

'It's not a joke,' Madeleine said. 'In fact, I think it's going to be good for us in the long run. You know how everyone is always saying how backward and irrelevant we royals in Preitalle are. We don't have quite the same standing as other European royals. But if we show how embracing we are of modernity it could make our future in this region so much more secure. Lucca Chatsfield has been at every high-profile party in England, Europe and America. He moves in circles most people can only dream about. Rock stars, celebrities, actors and film directors—you name it. Having him involved in the organising of my reception will heighten my popularity— I'm absolutely sure of it.'

Lottie rolled her eyes. 'How, for pity's sake, is a notorious hard-partying playboy going to help me organise a royal wedding?'

'Why don't you ask him?' Madeleine gave another one of her smug older and wiser sister smiles. 'Hear that helicopter landing outside? He's just arrived.'

Lucca had it all planned. He would pop into the palace, meet the party-plan princess and then hotfoot it out of there and leave her to fuss over the flower arrangements and the wedding fripperies while he laid back on a sun lounger on the nearest beach with a cocktail and a bikini-clad waitress by his side. Or three.

He'd done a little research on the trip over. The older sister and heir to the throne, Princess Madeleine, was known as the pampered princess. Not an out-and-out diva as such, but a young woman who knew her destiny from an early age and wholly embraced it. For years she had been squired by men from all over Europe but had recently become engaged to a studious-looking Englishman called Edward Trowbridge. Apparently Madeleine wanted a wedding reception extravaganza at the Chatsfield Hotel and had appointed her baby sister, Charlotte, as chief wedding planner.

He'd seen plenty of photographs of Madeleine De Chavelier in the press. She was a gorgeous, rather buxom twenty-six-year-old blonde with blue eyes and an extroverted personality that would stand her in good stead once it came time for her to take over the throne from her parents, Guillaume and Evaline. Clearly a favourite with the paparazzi, there wasn't a single photograph of Madeleine that could even loosely be described as unflattering. Fashion designers courted her, knowing she had only to appear in public once in one of their outfits and the item would sell out and a new trend would be set.

However, the same could not be said of Princess Charlotte. There were scores of unflattering comments about her lack of fashion sense, and some rather nasty and unfair, he thought, comparisons made between her and her sister. As if to back up their criticisms the press had sourced several candid shots that made Charlotte look severe and much older than her years. There was nothing about her private life other than one small snippet about a fling with a diplomat's son while she was at finishing school in Switzerland when she was eighteen. But if she had an active social life since it certainly wasn't wild enough to attract the paparazzi's attention, which, quite frankly, was a little intriguing.

There was nothing he liked better than to ride a dark horse.

'This way, Mr Chatsfield.' A palace official bowed as he opened a door leading into a morning room. 'Her Royal Highness Princess Charlotte will receive you now.'

The first thing Lucca noticed when he stepped into the room was a pair of startlingly green eyes glaring at him from behind a pair of tortoiseshell-rimmed spectacles. The princess was standing with her back ramrod straight, reminding him of a small tin soldier facing an imaginary battle. Nary a muscle on her slim framed body moved. It was as if she had been snap frozen...all except for a betraying little movement of her left index finger against her thumbnail, an agitated flicking movement that he suspected might have been an unconscious habit, like picking at a hangnail.

However, he could see why the press made such sport of her clothes. If what she was currently wearing was any indication, she either didn't have a clue what suited her or deliberately dressed in the most unflattering way possible. The below-the-knee plaid skirt teamed with a brown cotton blouse and covered by a cardigan that swamped her small frame made her look like a bag lady rather than a princess second in line to the throne. Her hair was neither blonde nor brown, but a tawny shade, and tied back severely from her face, giving her a prim, schoolmarmish look.

'Welcome to the royal palace of Preitalle, Mr Chatsfield.' She spoke in a coolly polite tone that had a hint of a French accent to it. She held out her right hand to him but he sensed it was out of a grim commitment to duty rather than any desire to make physical contact.

He took her hand and watched as her rain-forest-green eyes widened fractionally as his fingers wrapped firmly around hers, almost swallowing her tiny hand whole. Her skin was rose-petal soft and cool like silk. She tilted her head right back to keep eye contact with him, making him feel every millimetre of his six-foot-two height.

Her hand fluttered like a little bird inside the cage of his, sending a shock wave of heat through his pelvis like the backdraft of a fire. He released her hand and had to physically stop himself from wriggling his fingers to rid himself of the electric tingling her touch had evoked.

'Thank you, Your Royal Highness,' he said with exaggerated politeness. He might be an irascible rake but he knew how to behave when the occasion called for it, even if he privately thought it was all complete and utter nonsense. In his opinion people were people. Rich or poor. Royal or common.

She pressed her lips together so tightly as if she were trying to hold an invisible piece of paper between them steady. He wasn't sure if it was out of annoyance or a gesture of nervousness or shyness, but it drew his gaze like starving eyes to a feast. She had a bee-stung mouth, full lipped and rosy pink without the adornment of lipstick or even a layer of clear lip gloss. It was a mouth that looked capable of intense passion but it seemed somewhat at odds with the rest of her downplayed and rather starchily set features.

A feather of intrigue tickled Lucca's interest. Did she have a wild side behind those frumpy clothes and that frosty facade?

Maybe his exile here wouldn't be a complete waste of time, after all....

She stepped back from him like someone does in front of a suddenly too-hot fire. She squared her slim shoulders and crossed her hands over the front of her body, cupping her elbows with the opposite hands. 'I believe you have been appointed as my assistant.'

Lucca was seriously getting off on her priggish hauteur. It was so different from the way women usually responded to him. There was no simpering and batting of eyelashes. No breathy coos and whispers. No coy come-hither looks or pouting lips and delectable cleavages on show.

No, sirree.

She was buttoned up to the neck and spoke to him in clipped formal sentences and looked at him down the length of her retroussé nose as if he was something unpleasant stuck to her sole of her sensible shoe.

'That's correct.' He gave her a mocking at-your-service bow.

Her chin came up a little higher and those striking eyes flashed like green-tinged lightning behind those conservative spectacle frames. 'I think you should know that your appointment is both unnecessary and expressly against my wishes.'

Wow. Now *that* was some attitude.

He'd had every intention of leaving her to it but something about her stiff unfriendliness irked him. He wasn't used to being dismissed as if he was nothing more than a lowly ranked servant who had failed to come up to scratch. He was an heir of one of the richest families in England. He decided to dig his heels in. He wasn't going to let some hoity-toity little princess rob him of his allowance by dismissing him before he put in a day's 'work.' He would play the game for the sake of appearances and keep everybody at home happy.

'Your sister's wedding cannot go ahead without my family's cooperation,' he said. 'The Chatsfield Hotel is the only venue large and modern enough in Preitalle to accommodate a royal wedding reception.'

She gave him a defiant stare. 'We can have it here at the palace ballroom. It's what I proposed to my sister in the first place.'

'But that's not what your sister wants,' he countered neatly. It felt like a verbal fencing match and just as stimulating. He could feel the stirring of his blood, like a tapping beat picking up its tempo, taking heat to his groin like a spreading fire. 'The hotel is closer to the cathedral and she wants the neutral ground of Chatsfield to show how forward-thinking the royal house of Preitalle is becoming, does she not?'

Her lips compressed again. He could almost hear the cogs of her smart little brain ticking over. She was planning a counterattack. He could see the flickering behind her eyes as if she was mentally shuffling through her storehouse of comments to choose the most waspish one to send his way. 'I fail to see how a man who spends his life frittering away his time and his family's money on a profligate lifestyle such as yours could have anything to offer me in terms of services.'

Lucca smiled a satirical smile. *'Au con-*

traire, little princess. I think I have just the services you need to get this place rocking into the twenty-first century.'

Her cheeks blushed a fiery red but her mouth was still flattened chalk-white in disapproval. 'You do not have permission to address me informally. Please refrain from doing so. I am Your Royal Highness at first greeting and then Ma'am henceforth.'

'Would that be Ma'am as in schoolmarm?'

She drew in a sharp little breath and stalked to the other side of the room, still with her arms crossed over her body, her head at that proud height as she looked out of the windows to the formal palace gardens outside. Her whole body seemed to be vibrating with anger like a battery-operated toy set on an uneven surface. He could see her trying to control it, he assumed out of years of royal training. Presumably royals had tempers just like everybody else but they weren't allowed to use them, or at least not in public. But he had a feeling Her Royal High and Mightiness would give her best tiara right now for an opportunity to slap one of her dainty little fingernail-chewed hands across his face.

'I do not wish to have anything further to do with you,' she said in clearly enunciated tones. 'Please leave.'

'Listen, sweetheart,' Lucca said with a cavalier disregard for protocol. 'Way I see it, we're stuck with each other, at least for the sake of appearances. Your big sister seems pretty keen on us working together and I get the feeling that what she says around here goes. Quite frankly, I'd rather be working on my tan on one of your beaches, preferably with a couple of blonde beach bunnies peeling grapes for me. So kick me out if you dare. I'm cool with it, but you can say goodbye to using the Chatsfield.'

She turned and gave him a look one would do when a cockroach appears on the table in the middle of a formal dining setting. 'You are the most disreputable man I have ever met.'

'Looks like you need to get out more.' He gave her his fallen angel's smile. 'I can assure you there's plenty more out there like me.'

Her eyes slitted like a cat facing a feral dog, her hands balling into fists at her sides. 'Get out before I have you thrown out by my security team.'

He gave an indolent shrug as he ambled over to the door. 'I'll be staying in the penthouse at the Chatsfield if you want me.' He turned and blew her a kiss across his open palm. *'Ciao.'*

CHAPTER TWO

LOTTIE STORMED INTO her sister's suite of rooms a few minutes later. 'You cannot be serious. That man is insufferable! He's quite possibly the rudest, most uncouth man I've ever met. What can you be thinking to bring him here? I won't work with him. I won't! I won't! I won't!'

Madeleine slowly turned on the velvet-covered stool in front of the antique dressing table where she had been experimenting with a new eye shadow. 'You will. You will. You will. I want my reception at the Chatsfield Hotel. We've talked about it since we were children. I am not going to let a little personality clash ruin my fairytale wedding.'

Lottie loved her sister but she hated the streak of bossiness in Madeleine's nature. There were only three years' difference in their ages but once her older sister's mind was made up it was virtually impossible to change it.

But she was going to have a damn good try.

'Personality clash, you call it? I'd call it a personality collision! That man is nothing but trouble. He came swaggering in as if I was a housemaid instead of a princess. He called me sweetheart!'

Madeleine giggled. 'Did he?'

Lottie glowered. 'Not only that, he held my hand far too long.' She didn't mention the blown kiss. She was still too furious about that to put the words together. The audacity of the man was unbelievable. The effrontery of him made her blood boil. How dare he treat her like one of his shallow little strumpets?

'He's rather gorgeous, isn't he?' Madeleine swivelled back to apply dove-grey eye shadow to her left eyelid with a slim-handled sable brush. 'If I wasn't already taken I'd make a play for him myself. He's got that wild, bad-boy thing going on. That element of totally unapologetic outrageous wickedness that makes a girl go weak at the knees.'

Lottie locked her knees together just in case they took it upon themselves to be influenced by her sister's comments. Not that they hadn't already been influenced, not by comments about the man, but by the man himself. As soon as Lucca Chatsfield had taken her proffered hand something had ignited inside her body like a match struck against dried-up tindor. It had raced like a runaway flame right to the centre of her being and had sizzled there in secret ever since. His glinting dark brown eyes had roved over her like a minesweeper, taking in every nuance of her appearance. The mockery in his gaze had *infuriated* her. She knew she wasn't the beauty of the family, but did he have to rub her nose in it?

Schoolmarm indeed!

He was here to make trouble for her and she had to get rid of him as quickly as she possibly could. Her plans for a perfect wedding for her sister would be sabotaged if he got any say in it. He was an outright playboy. He didn't date women. He slept with them and then left them before they had time to put his number in their phone. The press was full of his wild-partying, hooking-up lifestyle. He hadn't had a single relationship that lasted more than twenty-four hours. He was a one-night-stand man. It was practically his brand,

for God's sake. What possible interest would
he have in planning a wedding? She would
be made a fool of and the whole world would
be watching to see it. *Argh!*

'You know he's not going to do a minute's
work while he's here,' Lottie said, jutting her
chin as she looked at her sister. 'He's only
here for show. He's using it as some sort of
layabout holiday. He was disgustingly blatant
about it. That shows how unprincipled he is.'

Madeleine picked up her bronzing brush
and swept it artfully across each of her regal
cheekbones in turn. 'Then perhaps you should
take him on as a project. Put him to work. Get
his nose to the grindstone and his shoulder to
the wheel or whatever the saying is.'

I'd like to get his back to the wall, Lottie
thought with venom. *I'd like to scratch his
eyes out. I'd like to slap his arrogant face.
I'd like to—*

Madeleine smiled at her in the mirror.
'Well, look at you, Lottie, love. I've never
seen you so fired up. He really *has* got under
your skin, hasn't he?'

Lottie quickly refashioned her features into
her customary ice-princess mask, although
inside she was still seething like a kettle left

too long on the boil. 'I can handle him. He's just a little boy who hasn't grown up.'

'He looks all grown up to me.' Madeleine gave a twinkling smile and waggled her neatly groomed eyebrows as she added, 'Or at least he did judging by that spread we saw of him in that London tabloid.'

Lottie flickered her eyelids in disdain and swung away. 'I do *not* want to be reminded of what that man gets up to in his spare time.'

'Then make sure he doesn't have any,' Madeleine said. 'Keep him busy with errands. You could do with a bit of practice at delegating. You know you have a tendency to over-control things.'

'That's because I've always found if I want a good job done I have to do it myself,' Lottie said. 'Every time I've trusted someone to do the right thing they let me down and I'm the one who ends up with egg dripping off my face.'

Madeleine made a little moue with her lips. 'You're not including me in that statement, are you, *ma petite*?'

There was no point arguing the point. Madeleine liked to think she was the model older sister. Nothing she ever did was wrong. Their

parents never criticised her because she had
always done well at school and didn't have
to study for hours to get facts and figures to
stay in her head long enough to recall them
for an exam. The press never found fault
with her. She never wore the wrong thing
or said the wrong thing or frowned at the
wrong time. She didn't bite her nails when
she was nervous. She hadn't caused a scandal
the first time she had been let loose at finishing school. She hadn't been taken in by false
charm and imagined herself in love with a
boy who had only slept with her because she
was a royal.

No.

Madeleine was perfect.

Lottie let out a long-winded breath. 'No,
of course not.'

Her sister turned around again on the stool.
'Don't you think it's time you loosened up a
bit? Got out a bit more, let your hair down?
It's been years since—'

'Don't.'

'You need to get over yourself. It's been—
what?—five years since Switzerland? You
won't even talk about it. Don't you think it's
time—?'

'That's because it's in the past and I want it to stay there.' Lottie gave her sister a cautioning look.

'Every time the word *Switzerland* is mentioned you flinch. There, you just did it again.'

Lottie pointedly opened the wedding planning folder. 'The last dress fitting is the week before the wedding. It's at 10:00 a.m. sharp.'

'But you haven't had a date since.' Madeleine was like a dog with a serious bone addiction. 'You can't lock yourself away for ever, you know. One bad love affair doesn't have to ruin your life. You're twenty-three years old, for pity's sake. You should be out partying and having a good time. You're missing out on the best years of your life.'

'I'm not missing out on anything.' Lottie said the words with what conviction she could summon. Although she had never been as outgoing as her sister, she hadn't been a shrinking violet either...more of a daisy that faded once the sun went down. But her first sexual relationship when she was eighteen had taught her a valuable lesson in trust. Finding pictures of her most intimate moments with her boyfriend on his phone that he had shared with his friends had bludgeoned her innocence to an aching pulp. Fortunately her father had been able to block any further circulation of the images but she had never been intimate with anyone since.

She told herself she didn't miss it. The sensual glide of flesh touching flesh, the heat and passion of mouth against mouth, the erotic glide of tongue against tongue and the release of pent-up primal urges were things she no longer allowed herself to think about. Passion was too overpowering. It took away rational thought and self-control.

The sensual part of her had shrivelled up and died from neglect…or so she had thought until this afternoon when Lucca Chatsfield's large masculine hand had encased hers. Trapped hers. Shivers of awareness had cascaded in showers down her spine like the dance of champagne bubbles poured into a crystal glass. She could still feel the stirring of her blood, the way it moved through her veins as if powered by high-octane fuel.

She gave herself a hard mental slap. The very last man on earth she would ever get involved with was a promiscuous playboy with fewer morals than a back-alley tomcat.

No. No. No. A thousand million, squillion, gazillion times no.

She would put him to work instead.

Lucca was sipping a martini—shaken, not stirred—when he heard a sharp businesslike rap on the door of his penthouse suite. He slipped his feet off the ottoman, stood, gave a full-body stretch and sauntered over to the door. 'Well, hello there, little princess. And bang on time too.'

The look he got from those green eyes would have felled a three-hundred-year-old elm tree at thirty paces. Her chin came up and her chest inflated on a deeply indrawn breath as if she were calling upon some inner reserve to confront him. He found her feistiness strangely endearing given her tightly controlled temperament. So buttoned up and yet positively steaming on the inside.

She was cute. Unique.

She had the sort of looks that grew on you. Not in-your-face beauty like her sister, but an underplayed elegance that was quite captivating the more he saw of her. She was wearing a different pair of glasses this time. A silver metal frame that was not as thick as the tortoiseshell ones, but they still made her look bookish.

'We have work to do,' she said without pre-amble.

'We do?'

Her mouth was tightly set as if she was holding an arsenal of stinging retorts behind the barrier of her lips and only just managing to keep them there. 'You are not here to party. You are here to help me. So help me you will.'

He leaned one shoulder idly against the doorjamb. 'Would you like a drink?'

Her eyebrows snapped together. 'Mr Chats-field, I am not here on a social visit. I'm here to assign you specific tasks to do with the wedding.'

'Humour me.' He closed the door and smiled down at her lopsidedly. 'I never do business with a clear head.'

Her eyes pulsed and flickered with such loathing he fully expected the lenses of her glasses to steam up right then and there. Or explode out of the frames. Her dislike of him was so intense and so palpable it made his scalp prickle and the base of his backbone tingle.

This was going to be much more fun than he'd thought.

She was full of passion and fire and yet she was so tightly wound up it made him all the more determined to press her buttons to see if she would explode like a firecracker. Was there a little bedroom firebrand behind that ice-princess thing she had going on?

She pushed the frames of her glasses back up her nose with a jerky movement of her hand. 'I never do business without one.'

'Then we're a perfect match, don't you think?' He took a sip of his martini and watched as her eyes narrowed even further in disgust. Little did she know it but she was fulfilling every schoolmistress fantasy he'd ever possessed. She made no effort to disguise her disapproval of his lifestyle and his personality. What would it take to get that tightly compressed mouth to smile at him or to yield to him in a kiss?

He couldn't stop himself assessing her trim little body with his eyes. She was wearing a classic knee-length beige linen dress with a thin black patent leather belt around her waist, and a matching black three-quarter-sleeved cardigan and low-heeled black court shoes.

Although reasonably stylish, the clothes were the wrong colour for her and made her look like a child who had raided her grandmother's wardrobe for a dressing-up game. She had a simple string of pearls around her neck and pearl studs in her ears, and her hair was still pulled back in that unflattering way, but it exposed her slim elegant neck where he could see a pulse beating like the heart of a hummingbird.

She turned swiftly and marched farther into the suite, stopping near the entertainment centre to face him again, her expression so frosty he was sure the temperature of the room went down ten degrees. 'Have you been to a wedding recently?'

'Nope. I generally try to avoid them.'

'What about your twin brother's?' Her brows drew together again. 'He's married, isn't he?'

'Separated.' Lucca took another sip of his drink and held it in his mouth for a moment. Orsino's relationship with Poppy Graham had always been a little complicated. He suspected there was some unfinished business between his twin and his estranged wife but he didn't like to cause any angst by asking too many questions. Although he was close to his twin, they lived quite different lives. 'They had a quickie ceremony five years ago. You might've read something about it in the press. It got quite a lot of coverage at the time.'

'I don't make a habit of reading such unedifying rubbish.'

He gave a little laugh. 'Nothing but the classics then, eh? Tolstoy? Hardy? Dickens? Dostoyevsky?'

Her eyes fired another round of loathing at him. 'What about your other siblings? Are any of them married?'

'No, none of us has been lucky—or unlucky, depending on your take on it—to meet their soul mate. Mind you, given the example our parents set for us it's no wonder we're all a little gun-shy in the marriage mart.'

There was a pregnant pause.

Lucca wished he hadn't revealed quite so much about his background, not that she couldn't read all about it online or in the gossip magazines if it took her fancy. People were still speculating on the whereabouts of his mother, who had finally walked out on the family soon after his youngest sister, Cara, had been born, leaving signed divorce papers on his father's desk. No one had seen or heard from her since.

The train wreck of his parents' marriage had affected all of his siblings in various ways. He liked to think he was the least affected but he knew it wouldn't take too many sessions with a therapist to see his inability to connect emotionally with people was a hoofmark of his childhood. He didn't talk about it. To anyone. He didn't even think about it. The bewildered little boy who had cried night after night for his mother was long gone.

Lucca's philosophy in life was to have fun. The only feelings he wanted were pleasurable ones, physical ones. He was a sybarite, through and through. He didn't deny it and nor did he apologise for it. He had been born to enormous wealth and privilege and he made the most of it. Exploited it. He didn't believe in working to live or living to work.

He lived to party.

He treated all his relationships as transitory things. Just like a party. He showed up for an hour or two, had a good time and then he left to move on to the next one. His relationships were simply casual hook-ups that had a common goal of pleasure, not permanency. He didn't set out to deliberately hurt people—he wasn't wired that way. He had suffered too much hurt in his childhood to make it his life's mission to do the same to others. He used them certainly, but he always did it with lashings of his signature charm so no feelings were damaged. He got in and out of relationships so adroitly the women he dated hardly noticed they were being dispensed with. The closest he got to commitment was keeping someone's number in his phone in case he ever fancied a booty call.

But as if the uptight little princess sensed his family background was a painful subject, or perhaps didn't feel comfortable offering a sympathy she didn't feel, she brusquely announced, 'I would like to inspect the hotel ballroom. I would like you to accompany me.'

It was the very last thing she would like, Lucca thought, which made him wonder why she had suddenly changed her mind about including him in the wedding arrangements when she had been so vehemently opposed to it initially. Had her sister put the hard word on her? He knew Princess Madeleine was determined to have a glamorous wedding with all the trimmings and there was no better place than a Chatsfield hotel to put on a party to remember.

Was little Princess Charlotte playing him at his own game? Making him tag along to every tedious meeting or boring inspection of crockery or cutlery until he got so thoroughly sick of it he walked off the job?

He wasn't going to let her trick him out of what was rightfully his. If he had to tag along, then he would, but he would make sure he had plenty of fun while doing it.

'Sure.' He put down his drink and gave her a winsome smile. 'I'm all yours.'

Lottie kept her back straight as a ruler as she led the way to the hotel lift outside the penthouse. She knew Lucca Chatsfield's dark brown eyes were following her every move. She could feel the lazy heat of his gaze sliding over her with every step she took. The man was a dissolute rake and she had no business in being even *vaguely* interested in his childhood with its tragic circumstances of a disappearing mother. What did it matter to her if he and his twin had been lost lonely little boys being brought up by their older siblings and a father who was known for his affairs and his heavy bouts of drinking?

Lucca Chatsfield was here for all the wrong reasons and she had to get rid of him by fair means or foul. She didn't want anything or anyone to jeopardise her meticulous planning of Madeleine's wedding. This was the most important month of her life. This was her chance to show not just her family—most especially her sister—but also the entire world she was not just the spare heir.

'Aren't you supposed to have bodyguards or something?' Lucca reached past her to press the call button just as she put her hand out for it.

Lottie snatched her hand back but not before it brushed briefly against his. She felt the tingle and sizzle of his touch travel straight to the centre of her being, pooling there in a hot liquid mass that seemed to take on a life of its own. She felt it moving through her blood, swirling, swelling, hot and urgent like a tide that was threatening to break its banks.

Everything about Lucca Chatsfield unsettled her. His easy smile, that knowing glint in his laughing, mocking eyes and his laid-back, couldn't-give-a-damn-what-you-think-of-me stance that was such a stark contrast to her straitlaced and serious demeanour.

He was a self-serving playboy, a time waster, a shallow sensualist with nothing better to do than swan around the globe from one holiday destination to the other. As far as she knew he had never held down a proper job and—unlike his twin brother, who contributed to charity through his thrill-seeking sporting activities—did nothing for anyone other than himself.

Lottie stared fixedly at the illuminated lights above the lift as it climbed from the lower floors, conscious of the scent of him, the energy of him, the sheer male overpowering presence of him. His potency seemed to reach out with an invisible hand and stroke her: her hair, making it restless at the roots; her breasts, making them tingle inside their lace cups; her belly, making it quiver as if he had traced its softness with a slow-moving fingertip right down to that secret place between her....

She cleared her throat, hoping her errant thoughts would take the hint. They didn't. 'I prefer to move about the principality without a security team unless it's absolutely necessary.' Her voice came out cool and clipped and formal while her insides glowed with heat like a ten-bar radiator. 'It's different when I travel abroad, but even then I try and play a low profile. It's my sister everyone is interested in, not me.'

'Does that bother you?'

Lottie chanced a glance at him to find him looking down at her with a studied expression on his face, his eyebrows drawn slightly together over his eyes. She completely lost her train of thought as her gaze meshed with that dark, suddenly serious one. She moved her eyes back and forth between each of his, transfixed by how deep a brown his were, so deep it was hard to tell where his pupils started and ended.

She let her gaze travel slowly down the length of his strong nose to his mouth.... *Oh, that wickedly sexy mouth!* She gulped back a tiny swallow as she followed the sculptured perfection of his lips. The lower one was much fuller than the top one, suggesting a powerful sensuality that threatened to melt her bones within the encasement of her skin. He needed a shave; his jaw was liberally peppered with dark stubble and her fingertips suddenly felt the inexplicable urge to see what it would feel like rasping against her skin. It had been so long since she had touched a man....

The pinging sound of the lift arriving at the penthouse floor jolted her out of her mesmerised state.

'No, of course not.' She elevated her chin. 'I've never been one for the limelight.'

'Is that why you dress the way you do?'

Her brows clanged together. 'What's wrong with the way I dress?'

He held back the doors of the lift for her with a strong forearm. 'You dress like you're going to a funeral of an elderly spinster great-aunt.'

Lottie glared at him. 'I'll have you know this dress is a bespoke design. It cost an absolute fortune. And just for the record, I don't have a spinster great-aunt.'

'That dress looks like it was designed for someone in their sixties. You've got great legs. Why not show them off?'

She stalked into the polished wood and mirrored cabin of the lift, turning to face him as the doors closed with a sigh and a hiss behind him. 'Why on earth would I want to do that? My legs are my business. They're not anyone else's. Just because I'm a princess doesn't mean everyone has to know what my legs look like. I don't want people speculating on how much cellulite I have or don't have or whether I'm fatter or thinner than my sister. Nor do I think it's anyone's business what I look like in a bathing suit or what I look like when I'm eating my breakfast or dinner or having a coffee with friends. I just want to be accepted for myself.'

The silence seemed to ring with the echo of her outburst.

Lottie looked at the floor, studying her toes in their conservative shoes with studious intent. For as long as she could remember she had always been compared, measured, against her sister.

Found wanting.

It had been unbearable in her teens; every photo call had been a form of torture for her. The press comments at times were brutal, especially to a young overly sensitive girl who hadn't yet found her social feet.

But ever since she'd come back from Switzerland she had tried to keep her head below the paparazzi parapet. She deliberately dressed down, even dowdily on occasion. It was her way of thumbing her nose up at the fashion set who thought she wasn't pretty or stylish enough.

She wasn't a beautiful blue-eyed blonde. She wasn't an extroverted butterfly that could work a crowd to her advantage, to make everyone love her in a heartbeat, to be dazzled by her and follow wherever she led.

She was a quiet mouse who liked to mull over things in solitude. To slip by unnoticed, to be in the background, to quietly get on with things that mattered without all the fuss and the fanfare.

'Must be a tough gig playing second fiddle all the time.'

Lottie looked up at him to find his expression was still ruminative. 'I wouldn't want to be playing first even if I had been born to it. Madeleine loves the fact that she'll eventually be queen. She's good at giving orders. I'm rubbish at it.'

'I don't know about that.' The corner of his mouth lifted in a wry smile. 'So far you've been pretty good at snapping out orders to me.'

'That's different.' Lottie stabbed at the ballroom-floor button with her index finger. 'You don't want my orders any more than I want to be giving them.'

He leaned against the wall of the lift, crossing one ankle over the other in an I've-got-all-the-time-in-the-world pose. 'I know what you're up to, you know.'

She hitched one of her shoulders in a guileless manner. 'I haven't the faintest idea of what you're talking about.'

He gave one of his low deep laughs that made her insides stumble. 'You're going to drag me to every mind-numbing inspection or appointment you can think of until I walk off the job in boredom. But it won't work.'

We'll see about that, Lottie thought as she pressed the floor to the ballroom again. 'What's taking this lift so long?'

As if to spite her, the lift gave a shuddering jolt and then hissed to a halt.

Fear scuttled up her spine like the sticky legs of a spooked spider. She stabbed at the button again. Frantically. Manically. 'Come on! Get moving, you stupid thing!'

'Looks like we're stuck.' He didn't sound too worried about it. In fact, his tone contained a hefty measure of amusement.

'Stuck?' Lottie rounded on him, her heart feeling as if it was beating inside her throat instead of her chest. 'We can't be stuck! I have things to do. People to see. A wedding to plan!' *I have to get out of here before I get into a claustrophobic meltdown!*

He pushed himself away from the wall of the lift to inspect the computerised control panel. 'We've stalled between floors.'

She glared at him crossly, trying to control her fear with anger instead of blind panic. 'You don't seem the least bit put out. This is your family's hotel. Doesn't it worry you that the lifts are faulty? That surely can't be good for your reputation.' She put her fingers up in quotation marks and put on a posh travel guide voice. *'Come to the Chatsfield and get stuck in a lift for hours.'* She dropped her hands and arched a brow. 'Not going to look too flash on the website, is it?'

'Not *all* the lifts are faulty. Just this one.' He leaned back against the wall again. 'This is a private one to the penthouse suite. I reckon you confused it by stabbing at the button too hard. You should try a softly-softly approach next time. Trust me—' his sleepy, half-lidded gaze slid over her like a caress '—you'll get way better results.'

Lottie ground her teeth. 'Thanks for the lesson in managing temperamental lifts, but don't you think you should do something like call someone for help? We could be stuck in here for hours.'

'What fun.' His dark eyes glinted, his mouth lifting in a slant of a smile. 'How do you propose we pass the time till help arrives?'

A tiny shiver raced over her skin. A different one this time, not of cold primal fear but hot primal attraction. The lift wasn't small by any means, but with him looking at her with those devilishly sexy eyes, and that wickedly tempting mouth smiling in that incendiary way, it felt like the space had shrunk to the size of a cereal box.

She could smell the sharp clean citrus scent of his aftershave, a mix of lemon and lime and some other exotic spice that intoxicated her senses like a potent drug.

She couldn't seem to drag her gaze away from his mouth. It was quite possibly the most attractive male mouth she had ever laid eyes on. The laughter lines either side of it only added to its knee-wobbling gorgeous-ness. Was that why women in their hundreds fell over like drunk dominoes whenever he beamed that bad-boy smile their way? He represented everything that was sinful and tempting, wicked and hedonistic.

Lottie swung around and stabbed wildly at the button again. 'I need to get out.' *Right now.*

He stepped up close behind her and cov-ered her hand with the broad span of his. Her heart did a crazy somersault as those long strong fingers touched hers, sending a cur-rent of high-voltage electricity through her entire body. 'Don't stab at it so savagely.' His breath teased the hair around her ears in a warm minty-and-martini-scented caress as he took her fingertip between his index finger and thumb and guided it to the button pad. 'Press softly. There, just like that.'

Lottie could feel the tall lean frame of him behind her from her cheeks of her bottom to her wings of her shoulder blades. She hadn't been so close to a man since...since for ever.

Her boyfriend in Switzerland had been a boy.

Lucca Chatsfield was unmistakably A Man.

Her senses were not just intoxicated—they were sloshed, smashed, stoned. His hand felt so strong around hers, it made hers feel small and dainty and feminine. His body was so male. She could feel its latent strength in his light hold and in the way his hard and leanly muscled thighs brushed hers from behind.

She could not get her brain to work. It was a swirling mess of jumbled thoughts. Wanton thoughts. Wicked thoughts. *Tempting thoughts.*

Was he going to turn her around and kiss her? Her heart banged against her breastbone at the thought of that sensual mouth touching hers.

Should she stop him or should she just go with it to see what happened? What would it hurt to have one little kiss? She hadn't been kissed in years. She had practically forgotten what a man's mouth felt like. Would his kiss be hard or soft? Rough or smooth? Would it be passionate or beguilingly slow and tempting? Would he taste sweet or salty? Warm or cool?

Yikes! He hadn't even turned her around and she could already feel the earth moving beneath her feet....

But then she realised it was the lift.

Lucca stepped back with a lazy smile as the lift doors glided open on the ballroom floor. 'What did I tell you, little princess? Softly-softly works like a charm every single time.'

CHAPTER THREE

LOTTIE MARCHED INTO the ballroom with her cheeks still glowing hot enough to cook a couple of eggs on. He was playing with her like a mean-spirited cat does with a hapless little mouse. Teasing her, toying with her, making sport of her to pass the time. He was mocking her for her gaucheness, *laughing* at her. He wasn't interested in her. He was playing a game. He was here under sufferance so what better way to amuse himself than to have a little flirtation just for the heck of it?

Softly-softly indeed! Nothing about him was subtle. He was blatant. Flagrant. Shameless.

And oh-so-tempting.

She knew what he was up to. She was a challenge he hadn't encountered before, but she would show him that there was at least one woman in the world that wasn't taken in by sexy chocolate-dark eyes, a silver tongue and a body built for sin.

She had to get him out of her hair before he tempted her to let it down…*and she knew just the way to do it.*

The grand ballroom was as wide as it was long, and decorated in a Venetian palazzo style with a high ceiling painted a soft shade of grey with ornate crown mouldings of white and inlaid with gold. A series of archways lined three of the walls with plush crimson velvet curtains, and crystal chandeliers hung like giant handfuls of glittering diamonds, sending prisms of light over the highly polished parquetry floor. It was a perfect setting for a wedding reception. It had the signature Chatsfield style, glamour and sophistication about it that would make any gathering a memorable occasion.

'Not bad, huh?' Lucca said.

'It needs flowers.' Lottie walked across the floor, turning in circles as she checked out the corbels where she envisaged vases of flowers festooning like floral fountains. 'Lots and lots of flowers.'

He took out his phone and started scrolling through his messages, presumably from all of his female followers on Twitter. 'Flowers aren't my thing. I'll leave that to your expertise.'

Lottie didn't tell him she had already discussed at length with the royal florist every placement of every bloom and petal. Instead she gave him a pert look. 'No, you won't. I need male input. I might make it too girlie or something. We can't have all the male guests feeling intimidated, can we?'

His eyes gave a little roll. 'God forbid.'

'Come on.' She turned sharply on her heel. 'We have work to do.'

'Where are you taking me?' To her delight his voice sounded a little pained as he put his phone away.

'To the palace gardens. I want to pick a selection to see what would work best.' She gave him a sugar-sweet smile over her shoulder. 'You can fetch and carry for me. Won't that be fun?'

The palace gardens were pretty spectacular even for someone who couldn't tell a rose from a ranunculus, Lucca thought. And early June was a fabulous time for any garden in the Mediterranean. Roses were in abundance everywhere, glorious fragrant bunches of them hanging in a sweet-scented arras over archways and trellises in a kaleidoscope of vivid colour. There were other beds of colourful blooms, old-fashioned cottage flowers such as sweet peas with a border of alyssum and lobelia, stately foxgloves and pink and blue larkspur, carnations and Canterbury bells and Queen Anne's lace.

Princess Charlotte was moving between the garden beds, stopping every now and again to pick a bloom with a pair of secateurs she had taken from one of the gardeners. She laid each bloom carefully in the flower basket she had hanging over her arm, and every artistic cell of his wanted to capture the vision of her on a canvas.

The late-afternoon sunlight cast her alabaster skin in a golden glow. Her eyes were as mossy green as the clipped box hedges she was leaning over as she snipped a blood-red rose from a bush against a stone wall. Some strands of her hair had worked loose from her tight chignon and were bouncing in tiny corkscrews about her ears. With the abundance of flowers in the foreground and the ancient castle in the background, she looked like she had stepped out of the pages of a fairy tale.

He took out his phone and selected the camera option. *Click.*

She suddenly turned and glared at him. 'Did you just take a picture of me?'

'Yes. It was a beauty. The light was amazing.'

She put the flower basket down on the flagstones and stalked over to him with her hand outstretched. 'Give me your phone.'

Lucca held the phone just out of her reach. 'What's the problem? It's just a photo.'

Her eyes glittered and burned with resentment. 'You had no right to photograph me without my permission.' She made a grab for the phone by doing a series of little leaps. 'Give it to me, damn you!'

'Whoa there, sweetheart.' He wrapped his fingers around her flailing arm to hold her steady on the uneven flagstones. 'You'll do yourself an injury bouncing about like that.'

She stamped her foot like a three-year-old child, making those cute little curls beside her ears bob up and down like springs. 'You are an odious brute!'

'I know, but that's part of my endearing

charm.' He loosened his hold a fraction. 'Now be a good girl and I'll show you how cool the photo is.' He brought the picture up and repositioned himself so she was standing shoulder to shoulder with him. 'See?'

She looked at the picture for a moment and then glanced up at him with a frown puckering her brow. 'Why did you take it?'

He slipped the phone in his pocket. 'No special reason.'

'I don't like being photographed.' She gave his fingers around her wrist a scowling look. 'And I don't like being manhandled either.'

He turned her wrist over and slowly raised it to his mouth so he could access the sensitive underside with his lips. He held her gaze as he brushed his lips against her delicately scented skin, watching as her eyes widened and her pupils flared like twin spills of black ink.

Lust heated his blood, set it moving, thundering, roaring to his groin as the tip of her small pink tongue darted out and swept over her lips, making them glisten invitingly. Her slim throat rose and fell as she swallowed; he even heard the tiny gulping sound in spite of the background chirruping of birds and the light whistle of the breeze moving through the cypress pines in the distance.

He lowered his head until he was barely a breath away from connecting with her lips, pausing there to give her the chance to pull back if she wanted to. He breathed in the sweet vanilla-milkshake scent of her breath as it danced over his lips as her mouth softly parted.

Come on, little princess, you know you want to....

The sound of the gravel being shifted by the tread of approaching footsteps made Lottie spring back from Lucca as if someone had fired a cannon from the battlements. She whipped around to see Madeleine coming towards them arm in arm with her fiancé, Edward Trowbridge. If the loved-up couple had seen anything untoward they were showing no sign of it; they were too engrossed in each other with their heads bent close together as they ambled along the pathway.

A tiny pang of envy twisted her insides. It would be so wonderful to have a man look at her with nothing but love and adoration in his eyes. No one would ever think she had romance running with wild hopes in her veins, but she secretly longed for a man to look at her as if his world began and ended with her. Would she ever find that sort of happiness? Or would she always be left on the sidelines, the spare part no one needed. The wallflower. The not-pretty-enough, not-smart-enough princess everyone either mocked or pitied.

Madeleine looked up and smiled. 'Ah, Mr Chatsfield, at last I get the chance to meet you and to personally thank you for stepping in at the last minute to help Lottie with the wedding arrangements.'

'It's my very great pleasure, Your Royal Highness,' Lucca said.

He was so charming, so adaptable to every situation, Lottie thought with growing annoyance. No wonder he had the reputation of being irresistible. That smile would melt through steel and leave it in a little silver puddle at his feet.

'How is she behaving?' Madeleine asked him once formal introductions were out of the way. 'She can be a little headstrong and overcontrolling at times.'

'Princess Charlotte is a delight in every

way imaginable,' he replied with consummate charm.

Lottie shot him a narrow-eyed little glare while the others weren't looking.

'Oh, you don't have to address her so formally,' Madeleine said. 'Family and friends call her Lottie. I'm sure she doesn't mind, do you, Lottie?'

'Not at all.' She stretched her mouth in a rictus smile.

Lucca's dark brown eyes gleamed with a wick of wickedness. 'Your sister was just consulting me about the flowers for the ballroom.'

'Oh, really?' Madeleine looked a little surprised. 'But I thought—'

'He's great at flowers,' Lottie said. 'A natural. Born to it. Should have been a florist. Missed his calling if you ask me.'

Edward Trowbridge's brows lifted ever so slightly. 'How…nice…'

'I thought she would've had you working on the entertainment program for my bachelorette party?' Madeleine said, swinging her gaze back to Lottie. 'What are you up to, Lottie? You're not up to mischief, are you?'

Lottie smiled innocently. 'You know me better than that.'

Madeleine swung her gaze back to Lucca. 'I'm afraid Lottie wasn't too happy about having any help with the planning at this late stage. She's a bit of a control freak. But this team effort will be really good for her. I'm sure you'll do a splendid job helping her to learn to let go a bit.'

'I'm putting in my very best effort,' Lucca said with a smile that would have charmed a seagull away from a food scrap.

Madeleine and Edward made their goodbyes and wandered off towards the grotto at the far end of the palace gardens.

'Nice couple.'

Lottie snatched up the flower basket. 'Just for the record, I would've slapped your face if you'd kissed me back then.'

'What makes you think I was going to kiss you?'

She stopped marching and rounded her gaze on him. Had she imagined his intentions? Was she so out of touch she couldn't tell when a man was interested in her or not? But whether he wanted to kiss her or not, she had been alarmingly close to pressing her mouth to his. Caught up in the moment she had been entranced, mesmerised by the thought of feeling his lips against hers. Her body had thrummed with the need to taste him. The teasing breeze of his breath against her lips, the way his breath had mingled with hers in that erotic way, had almost been her undoing.

'You...you weren't?'

He flashed a sudden grin. 'I was tempted, but I don't want to swing from the tower for breeching palace protocol. There are probably CCTV cameras behind every rose petal out here.'

She gave him a speaking look. 'I'm quite sure you wouldn't let the inconvenience of a centuries-old rule book get in the way of your base interests.'

He took the flower basket off her, somehow making the most of the opportunity to brush his hand against hers as he did so. The nerves beneath her skin leapt to attention, her stomach pitching in delight at the warm thrill that coursed through her body. 'So what's the penalty for stealing a kiss from a princess?'

She held his gaze with a spark of challenge in hers. 'Why don't you try it and find out?'

His eyes went to her mouth and then back to her eyes. Back and forth. Back and forth. *Will I or won't I?* he seemed to be asking himself. 'Are you flirting with me, little princess?'

'Of course not!'

He smiled again, a smug, self-congratulatory smile, as he flicked her cheek with an idle finger. 'You want me *so* bad.'

Lottie jerked back with a roll of her eyes, which she hoped would in some way cancel out her betraying blush but she wasn't putting any money on it. 'Tell me something…does your ego have its own zip code?'

He laughed as he fell into step beside her. 'Cute.' His shoulder brushed against hers as they went through one of the rose-covered archways and a shower of shell-pink petals fell around them like confetti. 'So…tell me why this wedding is so important to you.'

She gave him a sideways glance. 'It's my sister's wedding. Why wouldn't it be important to me?'

'Fair point.'

They walked a little farther in silence.

'I want it to be just as Madeleine wants,'

Lottie said. 'I want everything to be perfect for her.'

'Seems to me everything already *is* perfect for her.'

She glanced at him again but his expression was unreadable. 'Yes, well, some people are lucky in life and in love.'

'And you?' He'd stopped walking and looked down at her. 'Have you been lucky?'

'I could hardly complain given all this.' She waved a hand to encompass the palace and its surrounds. 'I never have to worry about having enough money for food or rent. I don't even have to wash my own clothes or cook my own meals.'

'What about love?'

She gave him an ironic glance before she resumed walking. 'That's a funny question from you.'

'Why's that?'

'You're a notorious playboy.'

'So?'

She stopped and looked up at him again. 'Are you saying you've been in love?'

'No.'

'Are you saying there is a possibility you *might* fall in love one day?'

'No.'

Lottie tilted her head at him quizzically. 'What, are you really saying you have no capacity at all to fall in love? None at all?'

'I thought we were talking about you?'

'I'd like to unpick this a little further first.' She put her hands on her hips. 'What is it about loving someone that is so terribly threatening to you?'

His dark brown eyes locked her out as surely as a shutter coming down. 'I didn't say it was threatening. I just don't think it's likely.'

'But why?'

'I'm not wired that way.'

'You're human, aren't you?' she said. 'We're all wired that way.'

'So when was the last time you were in love?'

Lottie had to give him points for outmanoeuvring her. She considered not answering but figured he would press her until she did. It was easier to be truthful and get it over with. She dropped her hands from her hips. 'When I was eighteen. But don't they say the first fall is the hardest?'

He shrugged noncommittally. 'Maybe.'

'I don't think I was really in love.' She fell into step beside him again. 'I thought I was at the time. I'd had a lot of boys interested in me but I chose the one I thought was the most genuine. In hindsight I could have chosen a little better. But that's teenage hormones for you.'

'It ended badly?'

'Don't all break-ups?'

He gave her another quick inscrutable glance. 'It depends.'

'How do you do it? How do you move from one relationship to the next without amassing collateral damage?'

A corner of his mouth lifted wryly as if he found the thought of it so remote it was amusing. 'I don't believe in hurting people unnecessarily. I think it's important to be honest from the get-go. I'm always straight about what I can and can't give. That way no one gets their expectations up. No promises are made so none are broken. No rings, no strings is my motto. I don't even hand out jewellery as a consolation prize. Waste of money.'

'I suppose that limitless charm you're so renowned for comes in rather handy when you're wriggling your way out of a tricky hook-up.'

He gave her a sardonic look. 'I thought you didn't read unedifying gossip?'

Lottie looked away from that devilish glint. 'Don't bother trying your charm with me because it won't work. I'm immune.'

She felt his gaze rest on her thoughtfully. She had a feeling that in spite of his layabout ne'er-do-well personality he projected, there was very little that escaped those intelligent dark brown eyes. 'How long since you had a lover?' he asked.

She turned swiftly to continue walking along the pathway. 'I'm not going to answer that.'

'You just did.'

Lottie tried to ignore him walking beside her but her body wouldn't allow it. Her arm tingled every time his shirtsleeve brushed against her and her heart would go off on another excited gallop. His tall warm presence so close to her made her aware of her body in a way she had never been before. She was livid with herself for being so easily unravelled by the first man who had showed an interest in her in years.

Gullible fool!

She had always prided herself on her cool inner reserve. She wasn't called the Ice Princess for nothing. She had taught herself not to wear her emotions on the surface, to let no one see what she was feeling, even though at times it made her appear much more formidable and starchy than she really was.

But something about this incorrigible rake made every nerve in her body come vibrantly alive. Every feeling she had locked so tightly away kept tapping on the door of its prison to be released.

Desire—a thing she had forgotten she even had the capacity to feel—was elbowing the other emotions out of the way, hammering with both fists, a hammering so hard it reverberated through her body, echoing the loudest in the secret cave of her femininity. She could feel it now—the slow ache of need beating with a primal pulse she could not ignore even if she tried.

She sent him a haughty look that belied the sensual tumult that was going on in her body. 'I don't mind you calling me Lottie in private but please desist in calling me those ridiculous endearments. I have no time for such falsity.'

He threw his head back and laughed his deep melodious laugh. 'You are *such* a cutie pie. I feel like I've time travelled or something. It's like spending time with a character out of a Jane Austen novel. Did you go to Prim and Proper School or something to learn to talk like that?'

She gave him a gimlet glare. 'Must you be so…so *annoying*?'

'All part of the service, milady.' He swept her a Regency bow before returning his glinting gaze to hers.

Lottie felt a reluctant smile twitch at her mouth. 'You are quite possibly the most immature and shallowest man I've ever had the misfortune to meet. Do you take *anything* in life seriously?'

He leapt up and gave a victory punch to the air. 'Yes! I did it! I made the prickly little princess smile.' He turned towards the palace, cupping his hands around his mouth as if to make an important announcement. 'Hey, everybody—'

'Stop it!' Lottie grabbed at his wrists but somehow he ended up wrapping his fingers around hers. She glanced down at the dark tan of his fingers overlapping one another around her wrists and her insides shifted like books being toppled off a shelf. Heat seared through every layer of her skin like a red-hot brand, igniting those glowing embers deep in her core.

His fingers tightened almost imperceptibly, as if he was countering any attempt on her part to escape the gentle handcuffing of his fingers. She drew in a scratchy breath as he closed the gap between their bodies without even seeming to take a step.

His eyes were heavily lidded, sleepy and unbelievably sexy. Bedroom eyes. I-want-to-have-sex-with-you eyes. His mouth came down and, with a whisper-soft press, briefly touched hers. It left her lips aching and tingling for more but he didn't prolong the contact.

He pulled back and smiled down at her, his eyes dancing with devilry. 'If I let go of your hands, are you going to slap me?'

Her chin went up again. 'Why don't you try it and see?'

His gaze went back to her mouth. 'If I'm

going to get slapped, then I might as well make sure it's worth it, don't you think?'

If he wanted an answer he didn't give her time to give one. Instead he swooped down and covered her mouth in a kiss that tasted of hot-blooded man and primal want with a generous garnish of ruthlessness.

The brazen thrust of his tongue as he entered her mouth made her heart rate skyrocket. But while that first thrust had been bold, he followed it up with cajoling sweeps and subtle dives that made her skin tighten and then pull away from her bones as it rose up in goose bumps.

He explored her mouth as if it were a dish he had never tried before and wanted to savour every moment of the experience. He took a gentle nip of her lower lip, pulling at it with his teeth in a playful tug that melted her resolve like a knob of butter on a barbecue. He stroked his tongue over her top lip, intricately tracing its curve, before entering her mouth again with a spine-tingling stab of purely sexual intent.

Her body was pressed so firmly against his she could feel every powerful throb of his erection against her belly. It seemed to resonate in perfect time with that pulsing ache in her womb. Her senses weren't just reeling; they were spinning out of control. Desire was a blazing fire inside her flesh, racing through the network of her veins, firing up every nerve and cell with combustible force. Her breasts felt acutely sensitive where they were crushed against the hard wall of his chest, her nipples tightly budded in response to her arousal. Her inner core was already damp and humid with want. She could feel the warm satin silkiness of it when she moved her body against the deliciously tempting friction of his.

His hands left her wrists and splayed through her hair, which somehow was now tousled about her shoulders instead of restrained behind her head. He captured a thick handful of it as he deepened the kiss. There was something almost primitive about his hold, like an alpha male ruthlessly taking control of the mate he had selected for his pleasure. It unleashed something equally primal in her. She nipped at his lower lip with kittenish bites, sweeping her tongue over it each time she released it.

He groaned deep in his throat and his hand

tightened in her hair almost to the point of pain. He took control of her mouth by covering it again with his, crushing her lips beneath the hot firm pressure of his. His tongue mated with hers in a sexy coupling that made her stomach drop like a desk drawer pulled out too quickly.

Her hands were around his neck, her fingers delving into the thick pelt of his hair, her mouth held captive by the mesmerising magic of his. *I want this. I want you. I want to be wanted.* It was like a silent mantra inside her head in perfect time with every thudding heartbeat that was sending her blood through her veins at a dizzying speed.

He suddenly pulled back and glinted at her with those sinfully dark eyes. 'Let's find a room. Your palace or mine?'

Lottie was jolted out of the sensual spell he had woven around her like a fist thrusting through a cobweb. *What was she doing? Where was her poise and self-control? One kiss and she was his for the asking?*

Not going to happen.

Did he really think she was going to dive headfirst into his bed just like every other woman he made a play for, only to have him dismiss her like a toy that no longer held its initial appeal? He looked so assured, so supremely confident. Arrogant. She would be just another notch on his bedpost; no doubt her royal status would be of particular appeal to such a shallow celebrity trophy hunter. She had learned that lesson before—the hard way.

She wasn't naive enough to fall for it again. Not any more.

But rather than give him the satisfaction to know he had got so far under her skin she decided to go along with it...to a point. It would be fun to have the last laugh, to score a few points against him.

Lottie put on a worldly look, even managing a coquettish smile. 'Your place. Shall we say in half an hour?'

'Make it an hour.' His dark eyes glinted again. 'I want to slip into something more comfortable.'

CHAPTER FOUR

LOTTIE WAS CONGRATULATING herself as she walked on the main beach an hour later. She could picture Lucca Chatsfield in his penthouse with a bottle of the finest French champagne in an ice bucket, the sheets on his king-size bed laid back in preparation, maybe even some rose petals scattered there. Some in-house scented candles burning on the bed-side table with their scent of bergamot and sandalwood. His lean and toned body draped in a Chatsfield blue silk bathrobe with its gold embroidered *C* on the right breast, while he waited for her to knock on the door to attend one of his legendary scenes of seduction.

She smiled as she thought of the minutes and then the hours ticking by. His frustration building, his sense of humour souring.

One up to you, my girl.

She walked the full length of the beach,

losing herself in the crowds of bathers and sunbakers who didn't recognise her in her tracksuit and T-shirt and trainers with her hair stuffed underneath a baseball cap. She looked just like any other sporty girl out for a brisk walk along the seashore. She could have gone to one of the more private beaches on the island but she liked being amongst the people, pretending she was normal, getting a feel for how different her life would have been if she had been born a commoner. No pressure to look perfect. No one commenting on her expression or outfit. No one befriending her just because she was royal and not because of who she was inside.

Lottie was walking past the bar area at the main tourist area when she caught sight of a lean and toned male body stretched lazily out on one of the sun lounges. The glisten of sun lotion on his skin made his body look like that of a bronzed god who had just stepped off a plinth at the National Art Gallery. His abdominal muscles were like tightly rolled bands of steel, his long muscled legs with their covering of coarse hair were splayed, showing the proud heft of his masculinity beneath close-fitting black Lycra bathers. There was a colourful drink on a table by his side with one of those little paper umbrellas in it, and on the other side of him was a blonde bikini-clad girl with a tray of nibbles bending down to him with a come-and-get-me smile and a cleavage you could park a pushbike in.

Lottie blinked a couple of times. *It couldn't be.* He was back in his room waiting for her to show up. She was teaching him a much-needed lesson. She was giving him a massive blow to his arrogant confidence. She was—

She frowned and peered a little more intently. Maybe it was his twin. They were identical so maybe Orsino Chatsfield had come to Preitalle and was sunning himself on the beach with blonde busty beauties waiting on him hand and foot. But then he reached for his phone as the girls screeched with excitement at the prospect of a 'group photo.'

She ground her teeth to talcum powder.

It wasn't his twin.

As if Lucca had sensed her looking at him he turned his dark head and smiled that gleamingly white smile. He even had the audacity to lift up his hand and give her a friendly come-and-join-me wave.

Maybe he didn't recognise her, Lottie thought

as she spun around and strode back the way she had come. Maybe he thought she was just another girl he could reel into his harem with the crook of his little finger. No one else had recognised her in this casual get-up. Why should he?

Her feet pounded the sand, faster and faster until she wasn't walking any more but running, her breath tearing at her throat like fingernails.

She stopped at the lighthouse to check to see if he had followed her but there was no sign of him.

He was probably getting that stunning blonde to peel his grapes for him, while taking pictures of her doing so, which would no doubt end up on his Twitter feed.

Argh!

'What have you got planned for my bachelorette party?' Madeleine asked at breakfast the following morning.

'Don't worry. I've got it in hand.'

'Have you consulted Lucca about it? I'm sure he'll have some fun suggestions to make it an event to remember.'

Lottie scowled at her sister. 'It's my job as

maid of honour to organise your hen party. I don't need the input from some unscrupulous playboy whose idea of entertainment would no doubt include a male stripper jumping out of a cake or something.'

'Sounds like fun.' Madeleine grinned as she reached for the orange juice jug.

'You can't be serious!' Lottie put down her cup of tea with a clatter against the saucer.

Her sister took the seat opposite and cradled her glass of juice in both of her perfectly manicured hands. 'You're always so serious about everything, Lottie. What harm would there be in having a little fun for a change?'

'So…are you saying you *want* male strippers?'

'No, I guess we can't go that far, but neither do I want a sedate tea party with boring old cucumber sandwiches and scones. I want to have fun. I want it to be truly memorable. I'm not going to get married again so this is my last chance to kick my heels up as a single girl.'

Lottie chewed at the left side of her lower lip. She had a brunch party planned…strictly speaking she couldn't even call it a party. She hadn't planned on copious amounts of alcohol. She wasn't sure if she could cope with a bunch of out-of-control girlfriends of her sister's running amok so she'd kept things... well, sedate.

Madeleine reached for a fat buttery croissant and then pulled her hand back and sighed. 'How do you keep your figure so trim? I've put on five pounds since I got engaged. At this rate I'm going to need a shoehorn to get into my wedding dress.'

'At least you've got boobs,' Lottie said with a despairing look at her own flat chest.

'You just need a decent push-up bra. Speaking of lingerie...would you be a honey and choose my wedding night finery for me?'

Lottie frowned. 'Why would you want me to do that for you? Isn't that something you should be doing?'

Her sister smiled a twinkling smile. 'I thought it would be good for you to do it. With help, of course.'

Help?

Help!

Lottie's gaze went to paper-thin slits. 'Whose help?'

Madeleine reached out again and this time took the croissant from the basket and tore it into bite-size pieces. 'I've asked Lucca to help you. He wants to go to Monte Carlo on Wednesday on some private errand of his. I didn't ask him the details. I got the feeling he didn't want to talk about it. He's a bit of a dark horse, don't you think?' She didn't wait for a reply but continued. 'I thought it would be a good opportunity for you to go with him. You haven't been off the island in ages and with him as an escort you won't have to bother with having your own security guard.'

'I'm not going anywhere with *him*!'

Madeleine finished chewing her mouthful of croissant before asking, 'Why ever not?'

'How can you ask that? I hate him! He's a disreputable rake.'

'What? Are you frightened he might make a move on you or something?' She picked up another morsel of croissant and popped it into her mouth and chewed. Swallowed. 'You should be so lucky.'

Lottie pushed her chin up in a gesture of female pride. 'As it happens he did make a move on me.'

Madeleine's eyes rounded with interest. 'Do tell.'

'He kissed me.'

'And?'

'He propositioned me.'

Madeleine dropped the piece of croissant she was holding, her eyes as big as the plate she was using. 'What did *you* do?'

Lottie gave a little toss of her head. 'I arranged to meet him and then I stood him up.'

Her sister sat back in her chair with a musing smile. 'Well, well, well.'

'Don't get any funny ideas. He's the last man on earth I'd ever consider having a fling with. He's got no morals. He's a man slut, that's what he is. He doesn't stay with women long enough to remember their names. You should have seen the girl he had waiting on him down on the beach. She was fawning all over him as if he was some sort of sex god. It was nauseating.'

'Listen to you.' Madeleine laughed. 'There's nothing wrong with having a little fling if someone takes your fancy. It's about time you put yourself out there again. Lucca Chatsfield would be quite a fabulous scalp to hang on your belt. I bet there are things he could show you in the bedroom that would make your hair stand up on end.'

Lottie glowered. 'That man is nothing but

a thorough nuisance. I can't think why you agreed to such a harebrained scheme to bring him here to meddle with my plans. He's going to ruin everything, I just know it.'

Madeleine gave her a teasing smile as she reached for another croissant. 'I think you like him.'

Lottie sprang up from the table. 'I hate him! I detest him! I swear to God if he was here now I would say it to his face.'

'Save it, *ma chérie*.' Madeleine wiped her fingers on a starched napkin. 'You can tell him at dinner.'

'Dinner?' Her heart gave a sudden lurch. 'Don't tell him me you've invited him to dine with us. That's taking things way too far.'

'Not with us.' Madeleine said. 'You and him. Alone.'

'*What?*'

'You can consult him about the hens' night. I've planned a private dinner for you both in the Green Room.'

Lottie gaped at her sister. 'Why are you doing this? Have you gone completely mad?'

'He's fun loving and dashing.'

'He's an outrageous flirt and an arrogant devil!'

'I know.' Madeleine smiled again. 'Don't you just love that about him?'

A palace official led Lucca to a private room in the west wing of the palace. It was decorated in various shades of green with a background of cream with trimmings of gold. A small antique dining table had been set up in front of the large bay of windows that overlooked the palace gardens, and a bowl of full-headed creamy roses was on a brass-inlaid cabinet nearby, their peppery, clove-like scent filling the room. There were two deeply cushioned sofas facing each other in the middle of the room in a cream brocade fabric with an array of scatter cushions. A cherry-wood glass-fronted bookcase was against one wall with a small writing desk and chair set in front of it with a quaint lamp that was casting an incandescent glow over the room. It was a comfortable room rather than a formal one. It reminded him of a sitting room/library in a stately manor in the English countryside, not unlike his family home, Chatsfield House, in Buckinghamshire.

Thinking about home—*why did he persist in calling it home when it had never been*

anything like one?—always made him antsy.
He'd spent far too many years of his childhood yearning for a home and family like that
of his schoolmates. Chatsfield House was one
of the most beautiful houses in the English
countryside but no one could ever call it a
home. It had no heart. No warmth. No soul.
And as for family...well, with his older siblings and his younger one with issues of their
own and a father who sought refuge in a bottle, it was hardly what anyone could describe
as a happy family life.

The official poured Lucca a drink and informed him the princess would be with him
shortly before bowing politely and leaving.

He checked his phone to see he had missed
a call from Orsino. He'd yet to talk to him
about Giatrakos and was faintly curious to
see how the Greek had attempted to co-op
his brother. It was hard enough to get hold
of his twin at the best of times, consider-
ing he was usually halfway up a mountain,
or saving starving children in some godfor-
saken place, so how on earth Christos had
contacted him was anyone's guess. When
Lucca dialled Orsino's number there was no

answer—*typical*—so he left a brief message without saying much about his situation.

Ten minutes later Lucca had paced the floor so many times he was sure he'd left a foot-deep trench in the soft carpet. Was this another game of Lottie's? He didn't like the tables being turned on him. *He* was the one who played and won. If Lottie thought she could manipulate him to walk out before the time was up she was in for a big surprise. Nothing and no one was going to make him relinquish his goal. *No one*.

He turned when he heard a light footstep at the door. Lottie was standing there looking very composed but he noticed she was doing that flicking thing with her finger and thumb. She was dressed in black from head to foot, which did nothing for her colouring. Her hair was scraped back in an even more severe style and she wore no cosmetics or any jewellery. There was a spark of defiance in her gaze, however, that alerted him that her choice of garb this time might well have been for his benefit. Even her shoes were something a grandmother with bunions would wear.

'Who died?'

Her brows met between her eyes. 'I beg your pardon?'

He waved a hand to indicate her outfit. 'Have you been to a funeral?'

That stubborn little chin came up. 'I happen to like wearing black.'

'You look terrible in it. It makes me want to rush to the nearest blood bank to order a transfusion for you.'

She walked into the room with her head high. 'If and when I want fashion advice from you I will ask for it.'

'I liked that tracksuit you were wearing on the beach yesterday. I almost didn't recognise you.'

Her cheeks were pink when she turned to face him, her eyes behind their glasses—the tortoiseshell ones—brittle with resentment. 'Did you enjoy your drink?'

'It was very enjoyable. The view was amazing.'

Her look was brimful of dislike. 'The beach or that blonde's cleavage?'

He gave her a glinting smile. 'What do you think?'

She flattened her mouth as if she didn't trust herself to respond in a civil fashion. She stalked over to where some drinks were laid out and poured a glass of water but he suspected it had more to do with her needing something to do with her hands than actual thirst. She turned and cradled the glass without taking a sip from it. 'How did you know I wasn't going to go up to your penthouse?'

He studied her tense little expression for a beat or two. 'I knew you weren't ready.'

'Not ready?' she spluttered, eyes flashing at him in indignation. 'What, you think it's only a matter of time before I jump into bed with you?'

'Your body wants to, it's just your head hasn't quite got around it.' He took a measured sip of his whiskey and added, 'But it will.'

Her hands around her glass tightened. 'Your overblown confidence astounds me. I have absolutely no intention of becoming another one of your pathetically shallow conquests.'

Lucca wasn't used to women saying no to him. In fact, he couldn't remember the last time it had happened. But something about Lottie's spirit of defiance fired his blood like a shot of adrenaline. It was ironic that even dressed as she was like a nun, his desire was rampaging harder and faster than if she was standing before him in a string bikini. Or less.

He wondered why she was so determined to deny herself sensual expression. He had felt such intense passion in her kiss. But for some reason she refused to allow her passion to have free rein. He saw it in the way she held herself, that tight, almost-rigid containment, as if she was afraid of her emotions getting the better of her so had to put them under lock and key.

She didn't kiss like a nun. She kissed like a wildcat in heat. He wanted to feel that hot little mouth again and not just on his mouth. His body stirred and stretched at the thought of her sucking him dry. Of her hands skimming over his flesh, teasing him, burning him up with feverish longing.

Sexual conquests had become a little too easy for him. He didn't have to work very hard to get what he wanted. It had even become a little too predictable if he were to be perfectly honest with himself. He had the seduction routine down pat—a smile, a charming word or two, a drink and/or dinner and then sex. It had never failed him in the past. It hadn't failed him that afternoon on the beach, although he hadn't taken up the girl's offer to meet up after her shift.

But while the blonde girl had been beautiful, she hadn't made his flesh zap and crackle and tingle the way Lottie's touch did. Even the unbridled dislike in her flinty green gaze turned him on. She loathed him with every ounce of her being but the chemistry that pulsed between them was undeniable.

'Bet it wouldn't take me long to change your mind.' He gave her a lazy smile as he took a sip of his drink.

Her chin came up, those cat's eyes flashing at him haughtily. 'You're forgetting something. I'm a princess. I don't sleep rough.'

'I'll be gentle with you.'

Her cheeks pooled with colour but her mouth was set in schoolmistress reproach. 'Is there no limit to your impropriety? We are here to discuss the business of my sister's bachelorette party.'

'Fine. Talk to me. What did you have in mind?' He held up a hand. 'No, let me guess. You're thinking cucumber sandwiches, Earl Grey tea and scones in the conservatory, right?'

She sucked her cheeks in momentarily, bristling like a pedigree Persian cat in front of an ill-bred dog who was trying to pull off Best in Show. 'You're wrong. I was thinking of brunch.'

'Same difference.'

She frowned in irritation. 'What's your brilliant suggestion, then? Something tastefully inappropriate, I suppose?'

His eyes gleamed with something dark and dangerous. 'Has this draughty old castle got a dungeon?'

CHAPTER FIVE

LOTTIE BLINKED, TRYING to ignore the cold dread that slithered down her spine. 'Yes, but I hardly see what—'

'Perfect.' He grinned at her. 'What better place to put a bunch of girls who want to kick over the traces?'

'Are you out of your mind?' She stared at him in horror. '*A dungeon?* For a hens' night?'

'Run with it for a moment. We could set it up as a nightclub for the night. Hire a DJ, get the girls to dress up in costumes and—'

Lottie clapped her hands over her ears. 'I don't want to hear this. *La de da*—' she raised her voice in a childish singsong chant '—*I'm not lis-ten-ing!*'

'Where's your sense of fun?' he asked. 'Come on, think about it. How much fun would it be to have them party down there in the dungeon? We could dress the waitstaff in black leather.'

She dropped her hands and clenched them by her sides instead. 'What is *wrong* with you? Next you'll be suggesting they carry whips and handcuffs and tie all the guests up.'

'Brilliant!' His dark eyes twinkled. 'I knew you'd get into the spirit of it. Your sister and her friends will have a ball. It'll be a night to remember.'

She gave him a withering look. 'Drunken debauchery in the dungeon? Yes, that's really classy.'

'I can see you in a skin-tight catsuit with over-the-knee black leather boots. And a mask that only shows your incredible eyes and that sexy little mouth of yours.'

Lottie suppressed an involuntary shiver as his smouldering gaze ran over her as if he were already picturing her leather clad. 'You won't be seeing me. It's a girls-only event.'

'Aw, don't be a spoilsport.' He gave her a sexy smile. 'Can't I have a private audience with you before the party kicks off?'

The rattle of the dinner trolley arriving was never a more welcome sound to Lottie's ears even though her appetite was non-existent...

or at least her appetite for food. A hunger of an entirely different sort was gnawing at her now. She felt it pulling at her low and deep in her belly. A soft, insistent tugging sensation that made her insides feel hollow. Her skin felt too tight for her body, her senses too aware.

The air contained a silent note of anticipation.

If only he hadn't kissed her!

Then she wouldn't be feeling this wretched sense of emptiness and longing. Kissing him had been like tasting the highest quality chocolate for the first time. She would never forget the warmth, the melting smoothness and the seductive, addictive taste of temptation going head-to-head with years of temperance. Temperance didn't stand a chance. It was like a moth trying to fight off a mammoth.

That wicked glint in Lucca Chatsfield's eyes had lured dozens of women into his sensual orbit. She would have to fight with every atom of her being to not become yet another one of them. He was so practised at seduction. Even the way he spoke was like a caress— the deep mellifluous voice with its well-bred English accent that now and again betrayed his half-Italian heritage over certain words. The way he slipped endearments in so casually, the way he smiled with that sexy tilt of his mouth, the way his touch was so electric and exciting.

Lottie allowed him to seat her at the table but tried desperately not to show any sign of the impact his presence had on her. She had dined with numerous guests at the palace over the years. She knew how to get through a meal without spilling food or wine or leaving ghastly silences unfilled. But something about sitting opposite Lucca Chatsfield was another story entirely. His knees were almost touching hers underneath the table. She had tucked herself well back in her chair, and had even surreptitiously edged it back a little farther from the table after he had seated her, but even so she was aware of those long, strong, lean legs just inches from her own.

She picked up her wineglass with the tiny measure of wine she only ever allowed herself. 'What do you do in your spare time, apart from partying?'

'Not much.'

She searched his features for a moment. His eyes had shifted from hers as he reached for his glass and raised it to his mouth to take a sip. 'Don't you ever get bored with doing nothing other than spend your family's money?'

'It's my money too. I can't help if it I was born into a wealthy family. I just take what I'm given and make the most of it.'

She frowned at him. 'But don't you want to do something with your life? Something meaningful?'

He gave her another one of his devil-may-care smiles. 'Like what?'

'Study. Train for a career in something. I'm sure you're not without a brain. You could do something, surely? What about volunteer work? Work for a charity? Set up one like your brother has.'

He gave a negligent shrug. 'I tried studying but I got kicked out of Cambridge during my second semester. I won't tell you why. It'd make you blush.'

Lottie blushed anyway as her imagination ran riot. She didn't like to think what sort of stunt got him expelled from one of England's finest universities but she had a pretty fair idea it would have had something to do with his prolific sex life. 'Are you good at anything? I mean, other than seducing women?'

He averted his gaze as he twirled the contents of his glass. 'I have a few hobbies. Nothing too serious or strenuous. I didn't inherit the ambition gene in my family.' He put the glass down and levelled a look at her. 'What about you? What do you do apart from smashing champagne bottles against boats?'

She pursed her lips. 'I do lots of things behind the scenes. I don't like the spotlight so I leave the showy stuff to Madeleine. I organise the palace timetable. Setting up dinners for visiting royals or dignitaries. Garden parties, guided tours of the palace, that sort of thing.'

'Boring stuff, then.'

Lottie pushed her tongue into the side of her cheek and inhaled a long breath. 'It might seem hideously boring to someone like you, but I happen to find it immensely satisfying.'

The edge of his mouth tilted upwards, setting off a mocking light in his eyes as if the same muscles were involved. 'Sounds like a riot. Getting all those unruly ducks in a neat little row. Day after day after day. Year after year after year.'

She shifted in her chair as his satirical

scrutiny continued. 'So I like order. Is that a crime?'

That same side of his mouth lifted in a lip shrug. 'You can't control everything in life. You have to leave some wriggle room for spontaneity. No fun waking up each day to the same old tedious routine.'

She gave him an arch look. 'I am quite sure no two days in your calendar are ever the same. Waking up every morning with a different woman lying beside you would almost certainly guarantee that.'

'Ah, but that's where you've got me all wrong.'

She tried to ignore the wicked gleam in his eyes but even so the backs of her knees tingled. 'Oh, really?'

'I never spend the whole night with someone.'

Lottie couldn't decide whether to show surprise or disgust. 'Why not?'

'Why would I want to? Once the sex part is over it's time to say goodbye. I need my beauty sleep.'

'So no post-coital hugs or pillow talks till dawn?'

He gave a deep rumbling laugh. 'No. Not my scene, I'm afraid.'

'Interesting choice of words.'

His smile was still in place but it had hardened slightly around the edges. 'Which words would they be?'

'You're afraid.'

The hardness moved up to his eyes like a screen of opaque glass. 'What would I be afraid of?'

'Intimacy.'

He pressed his index finger on to the table-top and made a game-show 'wrong answer' sound. 'Nope. I love sex.'

'I'm not talking about sex,' Lottie said. 'I'm talking about allowing someone to get close to you.'

'You can't get much closer than having sex. Or is it so long since you got down and dirty you've forgotten the moves? Do you want me to give you a refresher course? I'd be happy to oblige. I'll even do a house call—or palace call, I should say.'

Lottie gave him a quelling look. 'Do you really think I would sink so low as to indulge in a fling with *you*?'

'Whoa there, sweetheart, I didn't say anything about a fling.' He winked at her. 'Just one night of bed-wrecking sex.'

She arched one of her eyebrows. 'One *full* night?'

'Half.'

'You drive a hard bargain.'

He glinted at her again. 'You won't find anyone harder than me.'

She suppressed a shiver of reaction and hoped he didn't see it. 'I was being sarcastic.'

'Sure you were.'

'I was!'

He reached across the table and captured her right hand before she had time to snatch it away. He turned her hand upwards and traced a light-as-fairy-footsteps circle around her palm, all the while holding her gaze with the impaling sexiness of his. 'You think by hiding your assets underneath that horse blanket you're wearing you're going to stop me from wanting you?'

Lottie swallowed. His touch was like fire against her skin, his gaze like a searing laser. Her body was a pathetic traitor. It trembled and ached. It pulsed and throbbed. It *wanted*.

She pulled her hand out of his with a sharp little jerk. 'I hate to deflate that overblown

ego of yours, Mr Chatsfield, but I am *not*
going to be seduced by you.'

His smile was lazy and supremely confident. 'You want me so bad I can feel it from
here.'

She coughed out a disparaging laugh.
'You're mistaking disgust for lust. I loathe
you. You're the total opposite of the sort of
man I would consent to sleep with.'

'Describe him to me.'

Lottie beetled her brows. 'Describe whom
to you?'

'Your fairytale lover. Your dream date—'
that wicked gleam danced in his eyes '—the
man you'd drop your granny knickers for.'

Granny knickers? Did he really think…?
She might lean towards the conservative side
in her clothes but her underwear was another
story. What she wore underneath her clothes
was her private indulgence and there was
nothing whatsoever grandmotherly about it.
She chewed at the side of her lip, eyeing him
suspiciously. 'Why should I tell you that?'

He lifted a shoulder in one of his careless
shrugs. 'I could help you find a suitable can-
didate.'

Lottie recoiled in alarm. 'You mean like set

me up? Matchmake? A blind date or something?'

'I know a lot of people. I have connections. I'm sure I could find someone to fit your exacting standards.'

'Please don't put yourself to any bother. I'm perfectly capable of finding my own lover, thank you very much.'

'You don't seem to be having much luck so far.' He picked up his wineglass and deftly twirled it by the stem. 'Your sister told me you haven't got laid since—'

Lottie got up from the table so abruptly the crockery and glassware rattled. 'My sister has no right to tell you anything about me. I know you probably think I'm an uptight prude who is secretly desperate for a bit of passion but you're wrong. I'm perfectly happy with my life the way it is.' She put her napkin down on the table with unnecessary force. 'Enjoy your dinner. I hope it keeps you up all night with indigestion.'

'Aren't you going to show me the dungeon?'

'Ask one of the footmen to show you.'

'Frightened to be alone with me, little princess?'

Lottie turned to glare at him. 'I'm not frightened of you. I'm disgusted.'

He laughed as he raised his glass in a toast to himself. 'To pissing everyone off.' He knocked back the contents and then grinned at the empty glass. 'My favourite pastime… apart from sex, of course.'

Lottie could not believe he didn't care a jot for other people's opinion. Surely there was some small part of him that wanted validation. How could he possibly live his life so uselessly, so pointlessly? Was his life really about nothing but sex and sin? Surely he wanted more than that. Sex was good fun and all that but it didn't satisfy the greatest yearning of all. To be loved and accepted, to be cherished and valued.

He repulsed her and fascinated her in equal measure. He was everything she most loathed in a man. Reckless. Morally corrupt. Enslaved by his senses. Out of control. *Dangerous*.

But he made her laugh. He made her feel feminine and desirable. He made her *feel*.

She straightened her shoulders. 'I'll show you the dungeon if only to prove how unsuitable it is for hosting a party.'

His dark eyes gleamed. 'Will you hold my hand if I get scared of the dark?'

Lottie wondered if there was anything that truly scared him. He had such a fearless devil-may-care attitude to life, which—if she were to be perfectly honest with herself—she privately envied. She had let herself go just the once and it had backfired on her. Lucca let himself go all the time and didn't seem to care what the fallout was. He seemed to revel in causing as much of a stir as possible. 'Don't worry,' she said. 'We have electricity down there. It was installed ten years ago.'

He smiled that sexy trademark slant of his. 'If it fails, at least we have backup.' He glided an indolent finger across her cheek as if to prove it.

Lottie brushed his hand away but her skin was still tingling when they got down to the dungeon via a service lift that only palace staff had access to.

The door was locked but she knew where the key was kept. She took it out of its hiding place and handed it to Lucca. 'You can do the honours. The door's a little heavy for me.'

He gave her an assessing look. 'You're not thinking naughty thoughts, are you, *tesore mio*?'

Lottie hated that he could make her blush so easily. 'What naughty thoughts would I be thinking?' *Apart from getting naked with you and having the orgasm of my life?*

He was still watching her with a steady and knowing gaze. 'I don't mind being tied up or blindfolded, even whipped on occasion, but I draw the line at being locked in a dungeon all by myself. What would be the fun in that?'

'You have an overactive imagination.'

'So do you.'

Lottie rubbed her arms with her crossed-over hands. Aside from the danger of being alone with Lucca Chatsfield, she was seriously getting spooked hanging about in this dark corridor. It had been years since she'd been down here. Ten years to be exact. Madeleine had locked her in the dungeon as a joke when she was thirteen years old. She had been scared witless and had been claustrophobic ever since. 'Are you going to unlock the door or stand out here talking about it all night?'

He gave a low chuckle that echoed like a

villain's *muahhahaha* laugh in the cold dark space. She pinched her lips together to stop from smiling at his puerile sense of humour and stood well back as he unlocked the dungeon door. The hinge creaked like rattling chains and another chill tiptoed over her scalp like an army of ants with frostbitten feet.

'That hinge could do with a squirt of oil,' Lucca said. 'You ought to put one of your fancy footmen on to it.' He held the door open for her, sweeping his hand in front of himself to indicate for her to precede him. 'After you.'

'Um, you go first.'

His eyes danced. 'You think I'm going to fall for that old trick? Nah, you've got the wrong dude, baby girl. You go first. That way I can keep my eye on you.'

Lottie stiffened her spine and walked past him, the cold damp air wrapping around her ankles like the ghastly leg irons attached to the stone walls. In that terrifying half-hour when Madeleine had locked her in all those years ago Lottie had sworn she could hear ghostly wails from behind those ancient stones. She rubbed at her arms again and turned and faced him. 'As you can see, it's totally unsuitable for a hens' party.'

'I disagree and so does your sister.'

She frowned at him. 'You've already talked to her about this?'

'But of course. She thought it was a fabulous idea.'

Of course she would, Lottie thought with an ember of resentment burning in the pit of her stomach. Her sister thought she was a scaredy-cat and delighted in pushing her out of her comfort zone. Wasn't that the reasoning behind Lucca being brought in to add a bit of excitement to her staid and boring life? 'Yes, well, obviously my sister and I don't have the same taste in entertainment.'

'Or men.'

'I haven't told you my taste in men.'

'No, but I can guess.'

Lottie folded her arms. 'I'll save you the mental effort. Intelligent, hard-working and trustworthy.'

He rubbed at his chin thoughtfully. 'What about a sense of humour? Isn't that what women find most attractive in a man?'

'I prefer loyalty over laughter.'

'When was the last time you laughed?'

'I don't keep a detailed record.'

His gaze went to her mouth. 'Health experts say you should laugh every day.' His eyes meshed with hers. 'It's like sex. It releases feel-good hormones.'

Lottie wasn't sure how he had done it without her noticing but he was suddenly standing close enough for her to feel his body warmth radiating against her. Her heart skipped a beat as he traced the curve of her jaw with a fingertip. 'Wh-what are you doing?'

'I'm taking your mind off the fact that you hate being down here.'

'What makes you think I don't like being down here?' She'd tried for insouciance but was pretty sure she missed the mark.

He traced her lower lip with the same idle fingertip. 'You're as tense as a trip wire.'

'Maybe I don't like being down here with you.'

His eyes teased hers. 'If you didn't like being down here with me you would've stepped back ten seconds ago.'

Lottie stepped back so quickly she stumbled on the uneven floor and would have fallen except for the steadying action of one of his hands on her wrist. Her stomach hollowed as his fingers found the betraying leap of her pulse. 'Let g-go of me this instant.' To her chagrin her voice came out husky instead of brusque.

His fingers left a fiery trail over her skin as they slowly relinquished their hold. 'Don't forget our date tomorrow.'

She frowned as she rubbed at her wrist. 'Date? I'm not going on a—'

'We have to get your sister's wedding-night gear. I know just the place in Monte Carlo. A friend of mine owns an exclusive lingerie boutique.'

Lottie wondered what sort of friend. An ex-lover perhaps? He had 'friends' all over the globe. He was utterly shameless in how he conducted his life. He used people when it suited him and dropped them when it didn't. 'Why do you want to go Monte Carlo?' she said. 'We have perfectly fine shops here or we could shop online.'

'I have some business to see to.'

'What sort of business?'

His dark eyes twinkled. 'Secret men's business.'

Lottie glowered at him. 'A hook-up?'

'You could call it that.'

She clenched her hands into fists, struggling to keep her anger contained. Didn't he realise his outrageous behaviour would impact on her? He was making a game out of the situation but it was her reputation and her pride that was at stake. 'You're supposed to be helping me with the wedding. What will your father and his CEO say if they find out you're out partying on the continent instead?'

He leaned against the wall in that indolent manner he had perfected. 'They won't say a thing because you're coming with me.'

She narrowed her eyes to hairpin-thin slits. 'What? While you hook up with some balloon-breasted bimbo? I don't think so.'

'It's already arranged. Your sister's lady-in-waiting emailed me the details earlier. We'll fly over tomorrow morning by helicopter and spend the night at the Chatsfield Monte Carlo. It'll be a blast.'

Helicopter? *Ack!* The last time she had flown in one she had been wretchedly airsick and the press waiting near the helipad had got the most candid shot of her of all time.

But flying with Lucca Chatsfield was one thing, sharing accommodation was another. 'I'm not staying with you!'

'Separate rooms, of course.' He smiled an I'm-rotten-to-the-core-and-you-love-me-for-it-anyway smile. 'I'm to be your stand-in bodyguard. Reckon I can keep you out of danger?'

Why, oh, why was Madeleine encouraging this farce?

He was the danger.

Even if he didn't come anywhere near her, Lottie could just imagine the torture of listening to him having animal sex with some empty-headed wannabe starlet next door.

Argh!

CHAPTER SIX

LOTTIE HAD GROWN up surrounded by wealth, and was certainly no stranger to private jets and helicopters and luxurious hotels and palaces, but the Chatsfield Monte Carlo was one of the most stunning hotels she had ever set foot in. It had an old-world grandeur about it that made her feel as if she was stepping back in time to an era when glamour and style were paramount. Crystal chandeliers dripped like diamonds from the ceiling; the plush dark blue velvet sofas and chairs in the reception area were set on ankle-deep Persian rugs to soften the polished marble floors. Scented flowers adorned the reception counter as well as on a centre table in the foyer where a massive display of summer blooms sat in a glorious fountain of colour. Attentive uniformed staff moved purposely about the area, seeing to the needs of the designer-dressed and jewellery-clad guests.

Which kind of made Lottie regret her choice of clothes…

The passive-aggressive streak in her nature had made her wear her oldest faded denim jeans and a boring white cotton shirt, and seen-better-days-and-pavements black ballet flats that made her look like a midget next to the driver of the limousine, let alone Lucca, who towered over her like a skyscraper. She had her tortoiseshell glasses on and her hair was in a tight knot at the back of her head. So tight it had given her a headache, which had been amply magnified by the stomach-churning dread that had accompanied her on every agonising second of that flight. Fortunately it had been a smooth crossing but even so her fingernails were chewed back to her elbows. Not that Lucca had noticed. He'd spent the whole time flirting on social media. Damn him.

Beautiful people were everywhere. Male and female, young and old, dressed in designer clothes, the air pungent with the scent of expensive perfume. It made Lottie feel like a small brown moth in an exotic butterfly house.

She didn't belong.

Lucca glanced down at her once their luggage had been taken care of by a bellboy. 'You okay?'

Lottie gave him a pained smile that didn't reveal her teeth. 'Headache.'

A flicker of concern passed over his features. 'You should've said something on the way over.' He gently touched her forehead with the back of his hand like a parent would do a small child checking for signs of a temperature. 'I should've guessed you weren't well. You weren't snipping and snarling at me with your usual form. You barely uttered a word.'

'I'm not keen on helicopters.' Lottie wanted to kick herself for confessing it. She waited for him to laugh or make a joke of it but instead he looked at her with a tight frown.

'Why didn't you say? We could have come by ferry or hired a private catamaran.'

She gave a helpless shrug. 'I don't like confined spaces. They make me feel ill.'

'Come on.' He tucked her arm through one

of his. 'You can have a lie-down until you feel better.'

'Lucca Chatsfield?' A voice called out as footsteps click-clacked towards them as they waited for the penthouse suite lift. 'Lucca or is it Orsino? No, it's Lucca, isn't it? Can I have a quick word?'

Lottie mentally rolled her eyes. *Here we go.* The first of no doubt dozens of bimbos who wanted to burrow under the covers with him. She turned to see a woman of about thirty-five carrying a camera with a telephoto lens and a mobile phone.

The woman's eyes opened a little wider when she saw the way Lucca had Lottie's arm looped through his. 'Princess Charlotte? I mean, Your Royal Highness. Are *you* here with Lucca Chatsfield?'

The incredulity of the woman's tone irritated Lottie. Was it so unthinkable that a man—even a man as unprincipled and promiscuous as Lucca Chatsfield—would be interested in her? She tried to slip her arm out of Lucca's but he anchored her there with a firm press of his hand. 'No, I'm—'

'We're here on official business,' Lucca said with his customary charm. 'Princess

Charlotte isn't feeling well. I'm taking her up to bed.'

The journalist gave an I-just-got-the-scoop-of-a-lifetime smile. 'I'm sure she'll enjoy that.'

Lottie wrenched out of his hold once the lift doors had pinged to a close. 'Have you gone completely mad? What the hell are you playing at? She'll tell everyone we're dating!'

'So?'

'So?' She glared at him. 'So? You don't date. Remember? You have sex with women, then dump them before they get their clothes back on.'

He scratched at his jaw, the sound of his stubble rasping against his fingers loud in the silence. 'Mmm, you may have a point there. This could be very bad for my reputation.'

Lottie spread her hands, glaring at him furiously. '*Your reputation?* What about mine? It'll be over every newspaper by morning that I was whisked up to your penthouse like some silly little floozy who can't wait to get naked with you.'

His eyes ran over her jeans and cotton shirt, wrinkling his nose as if she were wearing a bin liner. A used one. 'Nah, they'll never buy it.'

She folded her arms across her chest and scowled at him. 'What? I suppose my breasts aren't big enough.'

His eyes went to her breasts, lingered there for a moment like a warm caress. 'Your breasts are fine.'

'Is it because I've got a working brain between my ears?'

'On the contrary. I find your intelligence a big turn-on.' His eyes smouldered as they went to her mouth. 'But then, I don't think there's a man alive who doesn't get off on a smart mouth and a quick tongue.'

Lottie felt a lava-hot blush creep up over her face. Heat flowed through her body like a flood of fire, igniting her core so that it pulsed and throbbed with a hollow ache that was shockingly primitive. Her mind had any number of reasons—literally thousands of reasons—to keep her distance from Lucca Chatsfield but her body had somehow lost connection with Ground Control. It was running on autopilot, wired to some primal frequency that had no relation to common sense.

She found herself wondering what it would

be like to taste him intimately. To run her tongue down the length of him, to taste the male essence of him. To feel him shudder and convulse and flood in ultimate pleasure. To feel his skin slick with sweat against her own.

He moved a step closer and brushed against her cheek with a fingertip. 'You really are burning up, aren't you?'

His pelvis was just inches from hers. She could feel the cold metal buckle of his belt against her belly through the thin cotton of her shirt. She could feel her pulse revving like a Formula One car on the starting line. *Broohm. Broohm. Broohm.*

Lottie didn't dare lock gazes with him. She kept her eyes trained on the V of his shirt where some dark curly hairs were showing. She knew she should step back. *Why wasn't she stepping back?* Her feet felt like they were stuck to the floor. 'Maybe I'm coming down with something.'

'Hope it's not catching.'

She looked at his shirt button. His chest hair was too much of a heady reminder of the potent hormones that were surging around his body. 'I'm sure your immunity is far superior to mine.'

He gave a light chuckle and stepped back as the doors of the lift opened. 'This is our stop.'

Lottie stalled outside the penthouse and eyed him warily. 'I thought you said separate rooms.'

'There's a separate suite off this one.' He held the door open. 'All the Chatsfield hotels have multiple-suite penthouses.'

'Do the doors have locks?'

'What?' He flashed a grin at her. 'Are you worried you might be tempted to gate crash one of my orgies?'

She gave him a gelid look. 'I hope my suite has a pair of industrial-size earplugs.'

'I don't snore if that's what's worrying you.'

'You probably aren't asleep long enough between switchovers of bedmates to get to the snoring stage,' she muttered.

He laughed as he tossed his jacket over the back of the nearest sofa. 'You're really good for my ego, *cara mia*. You make me sound like some sort of go-all-night superstud.'

She forced herself to look him in the eye. 'How many would you do in one night?'

He did that little lip-shrug thing again. 'Depends.'

'On?'

He undid another couple of the buttons on his shirt. 'Chemistry.'

'I guess we're not talking about the periodic table of the elements.'

His smile crinkled up the corners of his eyes. 'Don't worry. I'll try and tone it down. I might even abstain for the night.'

Lottie gave him a look. 'Long service leave?'

He screwed up his forehead as if mentally calculating the years. 'Yep, I reckon I more than qualify.' He scratched at his chin stubble again. 'Let me see now...my first time was when I was—'

She rolled her eyes. 'Please spare me the details.'

He scrubbed a hand through his hair, making it all tousled, which somehow made him look even more lethally attractive. 'You want something for that headache?'

'I don't— I mean, I think I'll just have a little rest,' Lottie said, backing away towards the adjoining door. 'What time will you be finished with your business appointment?'

'That's not until tomorrow morning.'

'But I thought you had to be here by today?'

She frowned as she tried to recall the conversation with her sister. 'I'm sure Madeleine said you had to be in Monte Carlo by Wednesday.'

'That's because I didn't want to leave anything to chance.' He rolled back the cuffs of his shirt over his forearms, focusing on the task with what seemed to her a rather pointed concentration.

'So this appointment is pretty important to you?'

He looked at her then but his expression was difficult to decipher. 'It's just something I've had my eye on for a while. No big deal.'

'Is the something you've had your eye on female?' Lottie wished she hadn't asked but the words had tumbled out before she could stop them.

A light of amusement twinkled in his chocolate-dark eyes. 'How'd you guess?'

Two hours later Lottie was led by Lucca into his friend's exclusive lingerie boutique in one of the cobbled side streets in the centre of Monte Carlo. The friend was female—of course—but at least fifteen years older than Lucca, which somehow made Lottie feel a little less peevish, but only just. He probably routinely slept with women old enough to be his mother. Maybe even old enough to be his grandmother.

Once the introductions and pleasantries were out of the way, Rochelle Talliarde brought out a range of items for Lottie's inspection. 'Did you have something particular in mind?'

'Um…' It was hard for Lottie not to blush surrounded by such intimate garments, especially with Lucca standing there watching her every move. 'Something white or cream, I think.'

'How about this?' Lucca held up a black lace corset with red bows and leather lacing.

'It's not very bridal,' Lottie said with a note of reproach.

'Not for Madeleine,' he said. 'For you.'

'Me?' Her voice squeaked in horror. 'I would never wear something like that.'

'I reckon you'd look smoking hot in it.' His eyes danced with mischief. 'Why don't you try it on?'

'I will do no such thing.' She turned and picked up the first thing her hand touched and then blushed to the roots of her hair when she realised what it was. She dropped the skimpy scrap of lace as if it were a tarantula.

'Wow, now we're talking,' Lucca said as he picked them up again and dangled them from one of his fingers. 'Crotchless panties. A bridegroom's wet dream.'

'Will you stop it?' she hissed at him, conscious of Rochelle Talliarde looking on with obvious amusement.

'We'll take these and the corset and that oyster-pink ensemble over there,' he said to Rochelle. 'Now, let's get your big sister sorted. What about this? And this? And this?'

By the time every garment was tissue-wrapped and placed in the boutique's pink-and-black signature bags Lottie had gone way past embarrassment to outright mortification.

'Madeleine is going to kill me,' she said once they were out on the street. 'Poor Edward will probably drop dead with a heart attack as soon as he sees her in that get-up. We're supposed to be buying a royal wedding night outfit, not an S and M costume for a brothel.'

He grinned down at her. 'Where's your sense of fun, *mio piccolo*?'

She flicked him a disparaging look. 'You're utterly shameless.'

'I know.' He said it as if it were a badge of honour. 'It's my trademark. My brand. Cool, huh?'

She stopped walking to look at him. 'Wouldn't you rather be known for something other than a salacious scandal magnet?'

'Wouldn't you rather be known as something other than a prudish little goody-two-shoes who doesn't know the first thing about having fun?' he countered.

The mockery in his gaze stung her pride more than she expected it to. More than she wanted it to. Her entire body stiffened, like a porcupine extending its needles in self-protection. 'I'm not a prude.'

'Yes, you are. And a coward. You got burned once so you've locked yourself away up in your princess tower where no one can reach you.' His mouth lifted in a cynical, teasing curve. 'You're scared. That's why you hide behind that priggish exterior because passion frightens you. Life frightens you. You frighten you.'

Lottie hated that he knew so much about her—the *real* her—on so little an acquaintance. 'Oh, and I suppose you think you're the one I should let my hair down for, do you?' She poked a finger to his sternum. 'Well, let me tell you something, Lucca Chatsfield.' Poke. 'You're the last man I would ever get messed up with.' Poke. 'Because that's what you do.' Poke. 'You mess people up.' Poke. 'You play with them and then you dump them. I don't think that's anything to be crowing about. You should be thoroughly ashamed of yourself.'

He brushed her hand away as if it were an annoying mosquito. 'I'm not. So get over it.'

Lottie nailed her feet to the pavement. 'You think I'm scared, but what about you? When are you going to grow up? You're just a shallow Peter Pan playboy who hasn't even got the maturity to live off his own means instead of sponging off his family's fortune like some pathetic blood-sucking parasite.'

The silence was so intense it grew teeth.

'Are you done?' His gaze was steely, his jaw like concrete, all except for a nerve that ticked in and out on his left cheek like the flickering of a faulty switch.

Lottie refused to back down. There was something incredibly invigorating about finally getting under his skin. He was always so charming and laid-back. Laughing at life. Mocking it and everyone as if he didn't care what they thought of him. But underneath that party-boy facade was a proud and angry man.

A bitterly angry man.

'No, I'm not done,' she said. 'It's time someone told you the truth instead of dancing around you and feeding your ego the way that bunch of social-climbing sycophants you surround yourself with do. Who are your real friends? Who knows you? The *real* you? Who cares about you more than your money? Who cares about you more than anything else in the world? No one, that's who. You're nothing without your family's money and you damn well know it. That's why you want it so badly.'

He drew in a breath that widened his nostrils like a thoroughbred stallion facing a challenging opponent. He took her arm in a grip that was iron-strong and marched her along the street through the knot of people who had stopped to stare at them. 'Keep moving and keep your mouth shut,' he said through tight lips.

She pulled at his grip. 'Stop it. You're hurting me.'

He loosened his hold but not enough for her to tug free. 'I said, *Shut the freaking hell up*. You're causing a scene.'

'You're not the boss of me.' Lottie knew she sounded about three years old but she was beyond caring. She even had the toddler pout down pat and the leaden dragging feet.

His eyes cut to hers in a derisive glance. 'Now look who's acting immature.'

'Jerk.' She poked her tongue out at him. It was probably a bit over the top but it felt so good to spar with him. Her body was zinging with exhilaration. It was like being injected with a heady drug. She didn't want it to stop. She had never told anyone off in her life. Maybe she should do it more often. It felt good to stand up for herself for a change.

His eyes were like black flint. 'Don't get me started on the insults because I bet I know a hell of lot more colourful ones than you.'

He pulled her through the hotel foyer, rudely ignoring the obsequious staff member who spoke to him on the way past. He stabbed at the lift button, and as if they dared not disobey him, the doors instantly sprang open. He pulled her in with him and the doors hadn't even closed again before he pressed her roughly back against the nearest wall as his mouth came crashing down on hers.

It was nothing like his first kiss. It was not a kiss of seduction but of punishment. It wasn't meant to induce pleasure but pain. It was as if the fury that was buried deep inside him had finally found a leaky outlet. It was gushing forth like a blown pipe, pouring into her with blistering heat.

Somehow her arms ended up around his neck, her body pressed so tightly against his she felt the swollen length of his erection pounding with want against her belly. She tasted blood, somehow knew it was her own, but instead of trying to escape she kissed him back, using her teeth and her tongue and her lips as if this was the last kiss she would ever have.

The passion that rumbled through her was a scary, out of control entity. It was a wild primitive side of herself she was terrified of letting loose but there was nothing she could do to restrain it. Desire streaked along her veins like a river of fire, making her flesh feel vigorously alive.

His hot breath and his sexy coffee-scented saliva mingled with hers as his mouth devoured hers with primal purpose. The faintly musky and erotic scent of arousal haunted the air. Goose bumps of pleasure prickled out over her skin as his tongue tangled with hers, driving deeper into her mouth, making her whimper breathlessly in pleasure.

One of his hard thighs came between hers, rubbing against her intimately, ruthlessly letting her know what he could do to her with just a single stroke of hard male muscle against her throbbing need. She gasped as she felt the tingling of her inner core, the exquisite tightening of her flesh, the greedy desperate little ache of her tissues that were already wet and weeping with want.

But then he suddenly pulled back from her with a muttered imprecation, putting the width of the lift between them. He swiped the back of his hand across his mouth and then frowned when he saw a small smear of blood on his tanned skin.

His eyes met hers, his expression dark and tight with self-disgust. 'I'm sorry.' He grimaced as if it physically pained him to say the words. 'That was unforgivable.'

Lottie tentatively passed the tip of her tongue over the tiny split in her lower lip. She saw him follow the movement with his gaze, saw the convulsive rise and fall of his throat that signalled his regret even more powerfully than his gruff apology.

But she wasn't quite ready to forgive him.

Not for kissing her so soundly. But for demonstrating how pathetically weak her resolve was against his practised seduction techniques.

Resolve? *Ha!* What resolve? Armour smarmour. Going into battle with him was like going into a fencing match with a soggy noodle instead of a sword.

Pathetic.

She was pathetic.

The lift doors opening gave her the perfect exit cue.

Lottie turned and walked out with her back stiff and her shoulders neatly aligned, her head at an angle even her overly strict childhood deportment tutor would have been proud of.

It would have been a textbook I'm-having-the-last-word-by-saying-nothing exit if she hadn't stumbled over the carpet on the way out.

CHAPTER SEVEN

LUCCA RIPPED YET another piece of paper off his sketchpad and scrunching it savagely into a ball, threw it at the wall. It bounced off and landed next to the pyramid of sketches he'd tossed there over the course of the evening.

For the first time in his life he couldn't get into the zone. Couldn't centre. Couldn't *anchor* down.

Drawing was the music of his soul but tonight the band had packed up and left. Throughout his life, whatever emotions he grappled with, whatever demons he wrestled, whatever ghosts he avoided, he did it with pencil or paintbrush. It was his way of purging himself of every foul feeling festering inside him. The meticulous concentration of miniature work calmed him. Whether he was doing the preliminary sketch, or painting with one of his finest brushes while he worked under a large magnifying glass, the painstaking process calmed him like a lullaby does a fractious child.

But not tonight.

He was angry. Angry at himself. Angry for allowing his control to slip.

Lottie had needled him and instead of laughing it off in his usual I-don't-give-a-damn manner he had reacted. Let her see a side of him he allowed no one to see.

Her little dig about him sponging off his family's money seriously annoyed him. Who was she to talk? What about all the silver spoons she'd been fed with over the years? It wasn't as if she had a big career path all mapped out. She lived her life *through* other people. Planning *their* events for *them*. She had no events of her own.

He had a right to his family's money. The security of wealth made up for the emotional wasteland of his childhood. The loneliness he had suffered. The shame and hurt of not having a mother who had loved him and his siblings enough to stick around. The wretched disappointment when yet another important event at school ended without either of his parents showing up. He would look at all the other children with their proud and indulgent parents sitting in the school auditorium during a formal assembly or awards night or on the sports field. He would search that sea of beaming faces, hoping for a glimpse of his mother, desperately trying to match a face to the Laurent's painting that hung at Chatsfield House. He would think it each and every time, even though he had no hooks to hang his hopes on: maybe *this* would be the day his mother would return. She would come to see him and Orsino. To cheer them on, to be proud of them, to show she still cared about them. His hopes would mushroom up in his chest until he could barely breathe. But then, like a sharp pin piercing the thin skin of a balloon, his hopes would deflate—flat, useless, empty.

He hadn't made the most of his schooling. He had acted out his frustration, kicked back at authority, deliberately sabotaged his academic potential as a way of punishing his parents for not caring enough to show even a modicum of interest.

He had been lucky to have Orsino, but a twin was not a parent, and nor were older siblings. Antonio and Lucilla, his eldest brother and sister, had filled in where they could, but like Nicolo, and Franco, the next brothers in line, they had issues of their own to deal with.

And then there was Cara, the baby of the family, who had no memory of their mother at all.

Lucca swore as he dragged his hand over his face. He hated thinking about his family. He hated *thinking*. It stirred up emotions he had long ago buried, shining a bright light on the dark shadows of his hurt. The illumination of his pain made him feel physically ill. He could feel it now...the dead feeling in his muscles, the lethargy that dragged at his limbs. The tightness across his forehead, as if his eyes were being pulled back in their sockets by hot metal wires.

He picked up his phone, scrolled past another couple of missed calls from his brother, but instead of returning the call or distracting himself with social media he found himself scrolling through his photo file instead. He came to the photo of Lottie in the palace gardens. The light had caught the top of her tawny head, dividing her hair into segments like skeins of spun gold. Her skin looked as pure as cream with just a hint of dusky rose on her cheek that was facing the camera. She looked young and innocent, untouched, unsullied by the stain of twenty-first-century humanity.

He picked up a new pencil and turned over a fresh sheet on his sketchpad and started drawing.

Lottie had been fine about spending the night alone. *Perfectly fine.* Anyway, it had been *exhausting* doing loads and loads of shopping. It had been enormously liberating to wander about without a bodyguard, especially since no press had discovered her. With Lucca's cutting remark about her goody-two-shoes personality still ringing in her ears she had bought outfit after outfit in a range of colours and styles just to prove she wasn't half the coward he thought she was. She couldn't wait to see his face when he saw her dressed in hot pink and wearing make-up and with her hair loose. Which was why it was kind of annoying he hadn't made any contact since their little spat.

It wasn't as if she'd been expecting him to take her out to dinner or a nightclub or anything. Perish the thought! She was perfectly fine about watching old movies on the large-screen television and ordering room service.

It had been very quiet next door, which was both a relief and a surprise. She'd expected to hear a boozy giggle or two as he brought a nameless girl back from a night-club. She'd strained her ears for the sound of clinking glasses or the murmur of voices, but instead she had heard nothing, which just showed how incredibly soundproof the walls of Chatsfield Hotels were these days.

But when it got to ten the next morning and she still hadn't heard a peep from next door or received a text from Lucca she started to wonder if he had stayed out all night. She paced the floor of the suite and fumed. How dare he leave her hanging? It would serve him right if he missed his important business meeting due to a massive hangover.

Lottie glanced out of the window and saw a cluster of paparazzi in front of the hotel. There was even a television crew. Her stomach knotted. She had pointedly ignored the newsfeed on her phone and the newspaper that had been delivered in the early hours of the morning and was still hanging in its silk bag on the doorknob outside the suite.

She could just imagine what utter rubbish the press were peddling. Fashion Tragic Ice Princess Charlotte Spends Night with Dashing Hot Playboy Lucca Chatsfield in Secret Lust Fest.

She turned away from the window in disgust. She would be laughed at, pilloried as usual. Pitied for being the ugly sister. Cinderella without a handsome prince to take her to the ball.

No one would be running after her with a glass slipper in his hand.

No one would be running after her, period.

No one was even checking on her to see if she was fine about being left all alone for hours on end.

Lottie went over to the adjoining door, staring at the lock she had turned over the day before. She felt an inexplicable compulsion to open it. It was like an out of body experience as she watched her hand reach out and touch the old-fashioned brass key. The shock of cold metal against her fingers wasn't enough to stop her turning the key with a click that sounded like a rifle shot.

The door was silent as she pushed it open. It didn't even whisper over the carpet.

The bright morning light from her suite fanned across the room like the V-shaped beam of a searchlight and a muffled expletive sounded.

Lottie's heart jumped as if it had been jerked by a tractor towrope but she didn't back away or close the door. The suite was in total disarray. It looked like a tornado had been through it. Or a crazed burglar. There were balls of paper littered over the floor and the bed was a mangled mess of sheets and naked male limbs. No female ones that she could see. Thank God.

'Get the freaking hell out.' The words didn't quite have the sting they should have had. Lucca's voice sounded flat, listless, as if he didn't have the energy to spit them out.

'Are you all right?'

Another curse came out of the strangled sheets. 'Peachy.'

Lottie pursed her mouth as she came farther into the suite. She stepped over a damp towel, her nose wrinkling in distaste as she caught the sour smell of vomit in the air. 'Serves you right for going out all night drinking,' she said. 'Did you know that excessive amounts of alcohol can actually permanently damage your brain? The repeated bouts of dehydration causes the brain to shrink.'

He lifted his head out from under the pillow he'd been sheltering under and cranked open one bloodshot eye. 'This is not a hangover. I'm sick.'

She folded her arms like a schoolteacher listening to a naughty pupil's creative excuse for not completing homework. 'Sure you are. Copious amounts of alcohol irritates the stomach lining causing acute nausea.'

His head flopped back down to the pillow. 'Whatever…'

Lottie frowned. He looked dreadfully pale and he appeared to be shivering. She could see the shudders vibrating his body like the rigors of a bad fever. She approached the bed and touched the back of his shoulder. It was roasting hot and damp with beads of sweat. 'You've got a temperature.'

'You don't say.' Sarcasm should have sharpened his tone but it was still flat and toneless.

'Maybe we should call a doctor.'

'Maybe you should get the hell out of my room.'

'There's no need to be rude just because you're not feeling well.'

He rolled onto his back, keeping his arm across his eyes as if to block the harsh sunlight. 'Give me a break, princess. This is not my best look, okay? I just need a couple of hours to sleep this man flu off.'

'What about your terribly important business appointment?'

He sat upright so quickly his face drained of what little colour remained. Lottie saw him sway as if his centre of balance was skewed. But then he threw back the sheet and stumbled towards the bathroom, banging his shoulder painfully against the doorjamb as he went. He didn't have time to close the door to protect his privacy. He hunched over the nearest basin and was violently, wretchedly sick.

Every compassionate muscle of Lottie's heart contracted. She joined him in the bathroom, grabbing a fresh hand towel from the rack and rinsed it under the tap before squeezing it out and handing it to him.

He pressed his face into it for a moment, his body still shaking with fever. 'Go.'

'I'm not going till I call a doctor.'

He dropped the towel in the vague direction of the bathtub. 'I meant to my appointment. You'll have to bid for me.'

Lottie scrunched up her forehead in confusion. 'Bid for you?'

He gripped the edge of the basin for balance as he looked at her through wincing eyes. 'I want to bid on a miniature painting. It's never been auctioned before. It's come from a private collection. The auction is at noon.'

'But I've never been to an auction before. I wouldn't know the first thing about—'

'Please.' His tone brooked no resistance. It was as if he had summoned the last remnants of his energy to convince her. 'I *want* that painting. It's the only one of its kind.'

She chewed at her lip. 'Do you have a budget in mind?'

Lottie had never felt more pleased with herself. She had not only got out of the hotel undetected by the press   thanks to the aid of a senior staff member, Jean Rene, who set up a decoy—but she got to the auction, which was being held in a private villa and managed to outbid the highest offer. The exquisite painting was no bigger than a brooch and was of the mistress of a duke from the seventeenth century. Back and forth the bidding went until it was finally down to her and a man in his sixties who eventually caved in, shaking his head in defeat as the auctioneer brought the gavel down. 'Sold to the young lady in pink at the back.'

Lottie got back to the hotel, again without detection, and dashed up to Lucca's suite as if she were bringing the crown jewels. 'I got it! I won the final bid. I—' She stopped and looked at the sleeping form of Lucca lying on the bed.

She put the painting down, along with the other three she'd bought, and went over to the bed. He was lying on his stomach with just a cotton sheet covering him from the hips down. She could see the outline of his splayed legs, one hitched a little higher than the other, the taut curve of his buttocks making something in her belly feel wobbly.

She reached out and gently brushed the damp hair back off his forehead. He didn't seem to register the contact. His breathing was deep and even, his mouth relaxed in sleep.

She waited a moment and then trailed her fingers down his cheek to see if his stubble was as prickly as it looked. It was. It scraped against the pads of her fingertips like sand-paper, making her insides give another little quiver.

She curled her fingers into a ball to stop them exploring any further and moved away from the bed. She let out a sigh as she looked at the chaos of the suite. She could call house-keeping but that would mean disturbing him. She could just as easily grab fresh towels and sheets from one of the housemaids and do a quiet tidy up and keep an eye on him while she was at it.

She gathered up the balls of paper and placed them in the wastepaper basket. But then her curiosity got the better of her and she bent down and took one out again and un-furled it. It was a rough sketch of one of the villas they had walked by the previous day.

She picked up another ball of paper and found another sketch of one of the cafés on the harbourfront. She knitted her brows as she took out yet another ball of paper. Each unfinished sketch seemed to tell her more and more about Lucca rather than the sketch itself. It was like peeling back the layers of an onion to find a treasure buried inside. She had never thought of him as an artist, and a remarkably talented one at that. The sketches might be rough but she knew enough about art to know he knew what he was doing with each stroke of the pencil against the paper. The detail and perspective were amazing. It was as if he was looking at the world with an intense focus, narrowed down to a minute degree to capture the hidden secrets of his subject.

But there was one more drawing.

Not scrunched up in a discarded ball on the floor, but on a sketchpad on the walnut desk over by the window. The pencil he had been using was lying crosswise on the pad, and an eraser was next to it surrounded by little rubber shavings. The antique chair was pushed back at a skewed angle as if he had got up in a hurry and hadn't had time to straighten it.

Lottie looked down at the drawing, her heart doing a little skip of recognition when she saw an image of herself picking flowers in the palace gardens. It was a work in progress, but even so, Lucca had captured something about that frozen moment in time, built it into a story that made her look ethereal, even beautiful.

She had posed for official portraits before

and had hated the stiff, formal results. She had always looked stuck-up and starchy.

No one had captured *her*.

She glanced at the bed. He was still soundly asleep, his chest rising and falling in slow deep breaths. Something prickly and tight in her chest loosened. Smoothed out. Flowed.

Escaped.

Lottie drew in a ragged breath and moved away from the desk. She set about briskly putting the rest of the suite to order. Work was a great panacea for wild imaginings that should not be allowed free. *Ever*. She was *not* to think of Lucca Chatsfield as anything other than an outrageous flirt, a layabout libertine who was only here to make trouble for her because that's what he did best. He courted trouble. He relished in it. The press documented it in colourful, lurid detail.

He was one big flashing human headline.

He wasn't the sort of man she should be thinking about. He certainly wasn't the sort of man she should be kissing, or touching, or sharing a continent with, let alone a penthouse suite, even if it had a hundred separate rooms.

And he definitely wasn't the sort of man

she should be fantasising about making love with, even though her body reacted to him like a magnet to metal.

Even now her gaze was drawn to him. He had rolled onto his back and the sheet had dipped lower, revealing a tantalising trail of black hair that arrowed down from his belly button. His abdomen was superbly defined, gorgeously lean and tautly muscled.

She swallowed as his hand absently started scratching at his lower stomach. She felt like a voyeur, getting off on watching him. Was there a man alive who looked more outrageously delicious? He had been wearing dark blue underpants when she'd found him earlier but she suspected he was naked now because she'd found a pair of underpants in the shower stall along with a used towel. She could see the contour of his penis, the way it seemed to swell before her eyes, as if he were dreaming of something richly erotic.

His hand went lower and Lottie abruptly cleared her throat, her face so hot it felt like it was on fire. 'Ahem. You've got company. Might want to keep that for when you're alone.'

His eyes opened and he blinked a couple of times as if trying to place her. 'Lottie?'

'At your service—I mean, not in *that* sense.' She waved her hands about the room, her blush deepening. 'I was just tidying up...a bit....'

He propped himself up on one elbow, his brow frowning. 'Did you get the painting?'

'I did.' She brandished it proudly. 'I had a ball—er, I mean, heaps of fun.' *What was wrong with her mind that it kept sinking into the gutter?*

'Good girl.' He lay back down with a sigh and closed his eyes again.

She gnawed at her lip for a moment. 'Are you okay?'

'Marvellous.'

'You don't look it.'

'Thanks. Appreciate it.'

'I mean, your colour's not right.' Lottie tentatively approached the bed. 'Have you had anything to eat or drink?'

'No.'

'What about if I get you something? Some light broth or one of those rehydrating drinks. I could call up room service if you—'

He cracked open one eye and gave her a wry look. 'Might as well tip it straight down the toilet and cut out the middleman.'

'That bad, huh?'

'Get me an eye of a needle and I'll prove it.'

She winced in sympathy. 'It's okay, I get the picture.'

There was a little silence.

'Thanks for getting the painting for me.'

Lottie felt a warm glow come over her. 'It was heaps of fun. There was this old guy there who was pretty determined to outbid me. I dug my heels in. I didn't care how much I had to pay, I was *not* leaving without that painting. It was such an adrenaline rush when it was over. I felt like I'd won a race or something. Can you get an endorphin rush from an auction, do you think?'

He gave her another one-eyed look. 'How much *did* you pay for it?'

'Um...' She pulled at her lower lip again. 'I can chip in if you think I overdid it.'

His mouth came up in a weak half-smile. 'I'm sure I can manage it. I'm a filthy-rich playboy, remember?'

Lottie gave him a sheepish look. 'About what I said yesterday...'

'I deserved it.' His gaze went to her mouth, his smile fading as his frown returned. 'How's your lip?'

She touched the tiny spot with the tip of her tongue. 'It's fine. I should use lip balm more often. Madeleine is always nagging me about taking better care of myself.'

His eyes meshed with hers, searchingly, as if he was trying to solve a mystery inside her gaze. 'I like that pink outfit you're wearing.'

'Thanks.'

'Why do you dress in such drab gear all the time?'

Lottie looked down at her hands, rubbing her finger over her bitten-down thumbnail in a circular pattern. 'It's a habit I got into. A way of giving everyone the finger about their criticisms of me.'

'The press?'

'Yes. And the public.' She met his dark gaze again. 'I've never been the picture-perfect princess like Madeleine. I don't think anyone's ever taken a bad photo of her. Every time there's a camera around I freeze. I feel awkward. I stiffen up. I can't act natural when I know someone's looking at me. And of course the press love those caught-off-guard shots without make-up or sweaty from the gym…or stumbling out of a helicopter looking green.'

'So you don't play ball rather than try hard and then get criticised for it.'

She saw something in his gaze she had never seen there before. Kindness. Understanding. She let out a slow breath and another notch of tightness in her chest loosened. 'That boyfriend I told you about? It kind of started with that.'

His frown shadowed his eyes. '*He* criticised you?'

'Not like that as such.' She picked at a rough edge on what was left of her fingernail. 'He took photos of me. Of us...when we were...you know...'

'And you didn't know about it?'

She looked at him again. 'Not until I saw them on his phone. He'd set it up on remote control. I was horrified. It was like a nightmare I'd stumbled into. I couldn't believe it was happening to me. He'd shared the photos with some of his friends. Luckily my father was able to pull some strings to stop the images going viral. You can imagine the scandal it would have caused.'

His frown was so deep it made him look ten years older. 'So you've pushed everyone away ever since?'

Lottie got to her feet and smoothed her skirt down over her thighs. She *never* talked about this stuff. To anyone. *Ever.* Why was she spilling all to Lucca Chatsfield, of all people? He'd had his latest bedroom antics splashed over the London tabloids the week before. He probably had an archive full of juicy boudoir shots. 'I should let you rest. I've cancelled our flight back. I think we should wait and see how you're feeling in the morning. Are you sure you don't want me to call a doctor?'

'No, it's just a virus. Hope you don't catch it.' He lay back with a weary sigh. 'I wouldn't wish it on my worst enemy.'

There was another silence.

'I saw the picture you drew of me.'

He didn't open his eyes but she thought she saw his body tense momentarily. 'It's just a doodle.'

'I didn't know you could draw like that.'

He made a dismissive sound.

'You're really talented, Lucca. *Really* talented.'

He opened that one dark satirical eye again. 'So if I asked you to come and see my etchings you'd come in a flash?'

Lottie gave him a prim look to disguise the track her mind was taking at his double entendre. 'I might appear naive but even I wouldn't fall for that hackneyed line.'

He gave her a rueful smile that had a tilt of sadness to it. 'You're a nice kid, little princess. You should stay away from bad boys like me.'

She put on a confident smile that took far more effort than it should. 'I intend to.'

CHAPTER EIGHT

LUCCA WOKE TO a raging thirst. He reached for the lamp switch, grimacing as the sweat-soaked sheets clung to his body like plastic wrap. He raked a hand through the stickiness of his hair and gingerly swung his legs over the edge of the bed. His stomach gave a gurgle like a drain but that was as far as it went. Thank God and all his minions.

After a shower and a shave he felt marginally better. Not well enough to face food but a glass of water went down and stayed down, which was saying something.

He picked up his phone and checked out the newsfeed. It was laughably ironic that every paper was carrying the story of him holed up in the Chatsfield Monte Carlo with Princess Charlotte in a love-in.

Seasoned Playboy Spends Second Night with Prim and Proper Princess.

Is This the End of the King of One-Night Stands?

Could Wedding Bells Ring Twice for Preitalle Royals?

He switched off the screen in irritation. What was it with these people? Who made this stuff up? Did they seriously collect a wage for such drivel? He hadn't even slept with Lottie.

She was not the sort of girl to have a casual fling. She'd already been exploited in the most appalling way. His insides twisted to think of how she must have felt to have her most private intimate moments exposed in such a sleazy way. He was pretty laid-back when it came to issues of modesty, but even so, any photos taken were with the consent of his partner at the time. He might be a little promiscuous but he still had *some* standards.

He picked up the drawing he'd started of her. He had to admit it was a good likeness. He'd captured that otherworldly look she had about her. It would look even better once he put some colour to it. That was the part he enjoyed the most, the detail going into a subject, the layers of meaning that each tiny brush-stroke laid down.

There was a light rap on the connecting door. 'Lucca? Are you decent?'

Good question, he thought. He hadn't felt decent in a very long time. Maybe never. He opened the door to find Lottie looking up at him with those clear big green eyes sans glasses. Was she wearing contacts? Her eyes looked particularly bright. In fact, all of her looked particularly bright. She was dressed in a sundress with bright yellow daisies on it, a wide white patent-leather belt cinched around her waist. Her hair was loosely tied behind her head with a matching yellow silk bow. She looked fresh and young and…decent. He felt like someone had sucked the air out of his lungs. He couldn't find his voice for a moment. 'Wow.'

Her eyes sparkled. 'Do you like it?' She turned in a full circle and the skirt of the dress lifted just enough to give him a tantalising glimpse of her pretty knees and slim thighs. 'I went shopping yesterday. There was this really helpful stylist at a boutique who showed me how to put stuff together. I maxed out my credit card. Actually, it was the paintings that did that.'

'Paintings?'

Her look was sheepish. 'I bought another three at the auction. I couldn't resist them. I'd never seen a miniature landscape painting up close before. Do you realise the incredible detail that goes into them? They look like a normal painting only smaller but when you look at them with a magnifying glass you see the amazing detail....' Her voice trailed off and her cheeks coloured up. 'But I guess you already know that.'

Lucca couldn't resist brushing a finger down the slope of her cheek. 'Are you always this bright and chirpy first thing in the morning?'

Her small white teeth momentarily sank into the pillow of her lower lip. His eyes went to the tiny spot where his mouth had bruised her and his chest flinched as if someone had just kicked his heart with a work-booted foot. 'Sorry, it's just I haven't felt this excited in a long time. I have my very own art collection. Of course, three paintings isn't much, but it's a start. Do you know of any other auctions I could attend?'

Lucca smiled at her fresh-faced enthusiasm. Smiled and yet felt that twinge of sadness he'd felt the evening before. She was so young, still a little naive. There were sharks out there that would circle her and gobble her up in a heartbeat. Only forty-eight hours ago he had been one of them. 'Sure. I'll email you some links.'

Her eyes drifted away from his. 'The papers are saying a heap of ridiculous stuff about us.'

'Yeah, I know. I'll have to work extra hard to get my reputation back in the sewer where it belongs.'

Her lips twitched as if she were holding back a smile. 'It's funny in a way. What they're saying.'

'Hilarious.'

Her smile broke free along with a little giggle that sounded like a tinkling bell. He had never heard her laugh before. He had never seen her dimples before either. They made her look adorably cute. 'I thought I'd be appalled but in a way I'm enjoying it,' she said. 'They think we've been up here swinging from the chandeliers when in fact I've been playing nursemaid and housekeeper. If only they knew.'

'I'm glad you've found the irony of the situation so vastly entertaining.'

Her eyes danced with what suspiciously looked like mischief. 'Apparently we're the new "it" couple. Madeleine called me to tell me my popularity rating is through the roof.'

Lucca frowned. 'You're not worried about your reputation being besmirched by being associated with me?'

She gave a little up-and-down movement of her shoulders. 'I've decided to get over myself. I've been hiding away for the past five years because some guy was a jerk. By staying locked away I'm letting him win. I've decided to come out. I want to party and who better to teach me how to do it than you?'

He held up his hands. 'Uh-uh, I'm not going there.'

She gave a little pout that did crazy things to his heartstrings. 'Oh, come on, Lucca. You do nothing *but* party. You'd be the best one to show me how to have a good time.'

Lucca found himself in the unfamiliar role of responsible adult. 'Listen, sweetheart, I'm not sure you're ready for the party scene. It's a jungle out there. You could get into all sorts of trouble.'

She smiled at him with a knockout sparkly smile. 'But not if I have you as my bodyguard.'

After talking to Lucca about her disastrous love affair Lottie felt a weight come off her shoulders like throwing off a heavy suit of armour. She didn't like admitting it but he had been right. She *had* been acting like a coward. Scared of life. Scared of stepping out of her rigid routine in case life threw up something she couldn't handle. How would she know if she could handle stuff if she didn't even try?

She had gone back to the dungeon and survived, hadn't she?

She had flown in a helicopter again and survived.

It was time to reclaim her life. She didn't care what the papers said. She was going to have a good time doing all the things girls her age would do. Dancing, drinking delicious cocktails, flirting with handsome men, kicking up her heels and feeling normal.

Lucca proved to be as wonderful an escort as he had been listener the night before. He hired a top model sports car and drove her down to Nice where they had dinner in a fabulous restaurant overlooking the beautiful turquoise blue of the water and the startling-white sand of the beach.

After dinner he took her to a nightclub owned by a friend of his. The music was loud and the patrons hip and übersophisticated, but after her second champagne cocktail she felt herself loosening up a tiny bit. But while Lucca went to the bathroom, his friend the barman insisted on her having a vodka chaser 'on the house.' Worried she might offend him by refusing, especially since he was Lucca's friend, she politely drank it.

It was like drinking a magic potion, an instant cure for introversion. The potent brew flooded her system, giving her a boost of confidence and gaiety. There would be no wilting daisy petals tonight. No way. She was ready to stand up and *party*!

She grabbed Lucca's hand as soon as he got back and pulled him towards the dance floor. 'Come on. Let's dance.'

His expression was more in line with an elderly guardian than a promiscuous fun-loving playboy. 'Do you think you should've had that last drink?'

Lottie couldn't remember feeling so deliciously relaxed. She hadn't had so much fun in ages. Probably ever. Her limbs felt all squishy and melting, and her usual inhibitions about dancing in public had completely disappeared. 'Don't be a spoilsport. I'm supposed to be letting my hair down. Why are you acting so headmasterish all of a sudden?'

He rolled his eyes and allowed her to tug him to the cluster of gyrating bodies. 'One dance and then I'm taking you home to bed.'

She swayed on her feet and tried to focus on one of the two of him that had appeared in front of her gaze. She couldn't work out if it was because she wasn't wearing her glasses or the third drink she'd had. Maybe a bit of both. 'Ooo, that sounds like *glooorious* fun. Do you really mean it?'

His brows snapped together in a frown. 'You're drunk.'

She tiptoed two of her fingers from his sternum up to his chin but her fingers weren't travelling in a straight line. 'Do you think I wouldn't want you if I wasn't a leetle teeny bit tipsy?'

He captured her fingers before they could get to his mouth. 'I'm not sleeping with you, Lottie. Drunk or sober.'

She made a little moue with her mouth. 'I know you want me. That day we kissed—'

'Was a mistake that won't be repeated,' he said in a clipped tone.

'I liked you being rough with me.' She pressed up against him brazenly. 'It made me go all fizzy inside. I've never felt like that before. I thought I was going to come on the spot.'

'Will you *shut up*, for God's sake?' His expression had gone from stern to exasperated.

Lottie giggled and wriggled her hips against him again. 'I've never done it with a partner. Come, I mean. I've only pretended. I'm really good at it. I bet you couldn't tell the difference. Do you want to hear me?'

Lucca swung her so quickly towards the exit she tottered on her skyscraper heels. 'Not right now,' he muttered.

'I know why you don't want to sleep with me. You're worried you might want to sleep with me more than once, aren't you?' Lottie was enjoying this newfound freedom of speech. She could say whatever thought popped into her mind and she didn't blush or cringe in embarrassment. 'You might want to have a proper fling with me, like for weeks and weeks, maybe even months and months.' She grinned at both of him. 'You might even fall in love with me like it says in the paper. Wouldn't that be a hoot?'

He let out a very rude word and tugged her towards the car.

Lucca carried the now-sleeping Lottie into the hotel. It was a relief to have her finally shut up. He couldn't imagine what the paparazzi would make of her tipsy ramblings about him falling in love with her. *Sheesh!* Luckily there was no one about. In fact, the place looked a little deserted. There weren't the usual crowds of guests checking in or checking out or people having drinks in the bar. It looked like a ghost-town hotel instead of the usual hub of activity even though it was only just past midnight.

A staff member came over hurriedly. 'Oh, dear, Mr Chatsfield, is Her Royal Highness unwell too?'

'No, just a little, er...tired. I'm taking her up to—to the suite.'

'We left several messages on your phone,' the man said. 'We've had to quarantine the hotel.'

'What?'

'There's been an outbreak of a virus.' The staff member gave a very good impression of hand wringing. 'The medical authorities want to keep things contained until they identify the cause. We're not sure if it's food poisoning or a highly contagious rotor virus. We're not taking any more bookings until we know for sure and we've been advised to keep all the guests on-site for forty-eight hours to stop the spread of infection.'

Lucca mentally rolled his eyes. He'd planned to fly back to Preitalle as early as possible the next morning. He didn't want Lottie under the same roof as him in case he was tempted beyond his endurance. 'Do my father and his CEO know about this?'

'Yes, we've informed them both. They've probably been trying to contact you. Have you had your phone off?'

'On silent.' Lucca hadn't wanted to face the fallout from his father or Christos when the news broke of his 'affair' with Lottie. He could just imagine the spraying he would get.

Not that he wanted their approval. Far from it. He enjoyed creating drama. It served them right for trying to control him.

Lottie opened her eyes and blinked at him owlishly. 'Have I been sleeping?'

'Yes, *cara mia*,' Lucca said, conscious of the staff member watching intently.

'I had the bestest time, Jean Rene,' Lottie said to the staff member who had remained nameless to Lucca up until that point. 'Lucca took me dancing. I had champagne cocktails that tasted yummy scrummy. And I had my first ever vodka chaser.'

Jean Rene to his credit didn't blink an eye. 'That is wonderful, Your Royal Highness. I'm so glad you had a good time.'

'I had a *marvellous* time!' Lottie crowed as she seesawed her lower legs up and down like an excited child while Lucca tried to hold her steady in case he popped a disc. 'Lucca's in love with me, aren't you, Lucca?'

'But of course, *ma petite*,' he said, mentally grinding his teeth.

She touched his bottom lip with her salty fingertip. 'You can't resist me, can you? I'm not like your usual floozies. I've got class.'

'You sure do, baby girl.' He edged towards

the lifts. 'Keep me posted on the situation, er, Jean Rene, okay?'

'Yes, sir.' Jean Rene smiled a man-to-man smile. 'Have a wonderful night.'

Lottie woke up with a blinding headache and a mouth that felt like she'd been sucking on a gym sock. She gingerly sat upright, wincing as the morning light threatened to laser her eyeballs. She reached for her glasses and blinked a couple of times to clear her vision.

Lucca was sitting in a wing chair in her suite…slumped would be more accurate. He was soundly asleep, his head lolled to one side, his feet crossed over at the ankles. He was still in the clothes he had been wearing last night; the top three buttons of his shirt were undone showing a rather delicious display of hard male muscle and wiry chest hair.

Why had he spent the night watching her sleep? Had he put her to bed? She looked down at her bra and knickers. *Had he undressed her?* She frowned as she tried to recall last night…. It was all a bit of a blur. A nice blur, however. She knew she'd had a good time. Lucca had been wonderful company. He'd made her laugh and he'd taken her dancing.

She carefully swung her legs over the side of the bed and tested her balance. Her head swam a little but she didn't feel too bad, all things considered. Nothing a hot shower couldn't fix.

She came out of the bathroom a few minutes later to find Lucca going through his messages on his phone. He looked up as she came in, his gaze running over her dressed in the hotel bathrobe and her hair in a towel turban on her head. 'How's your head?'

'Did you undress me last night?'

'Yes, but I didn't lay a finger—'

'Why not?'

He frowned at her. 'What do you mean "why not?" You were off your face, that's why not.'

Lottie tilted her head at him. 'I never took you for the chivalrous type. I thought you'd make the most of an easy lay.'

He stood and shoved his phone in his trouser pocket, his expression tight with reproach. 'There's something you need to learn, young lady. You don't need to be drunk to have a good time. You don't know what sort of creeps are out there waiting to take advantage of you.'

'Don't you find me attractive?' Lottie knew she was revealing her insecurities by asking but she couldn't seem to help it. He'd had the perfect opportunity to seduce her and he hadn't done so. Surely he'd had a little grope? Stolen a kiss?

He raked a hand through his hair and turned swiftly to leave. 'I'm not having this conversation.'

'Why did you spend the night in my room?'

He drew in an audible breath and swung back to look at her. 'I was worried about you. You were acting a little out of character, to put it mildly.'

'I wasn't *that* tipsy...was I?'

He gave her a hardened look. 'You were pretty smashed.'

Lottie screwed up her face for a moment. 'I don't remember much after that vodka chaser.' She relaxed her features into a bright smile. 'The nice man behind the bar—your friend—gave it to me on the house. Wasn't that sweet of him?'

His expression still had that pained tinge to

it. 'I'd stay away from champagne cocktails and men you don't know in future.'

'How I am going to meet anyone new if I only associate with people I know?'

'Not my problem.' He strode to the connecting door. 'I'm going to have a shower.'

'So, what time do we leave?'

He turned back to look at her, his mouth pressed into a thin flat line. 'We don't.'

CHAPTER NINE

'QUARANTINED?' LOTTIE GASPED once Lucca had filled her in. 'Does that mean we can't leave our rooms?'

'Apparently so.' He scraped a hand through his hair, a habit he'd developed recently, she'd noticed. That and frowning so deeply his brows met in the middle. 'They want to keep the virus—if that's what it is—contained.'

'Gosh, no wonder you looked so ghastly the other night,' she said. 'And here I was thinking it was self-inflicted.'

He gave her a levelling look. 'I know I've got a reputation for hard partying but I never let myself get out of control. I know my limits and I stay within them, unlike someone I know who shall remain nameless.'

'There's no point going on and on about it,' Lottie said with a cross look. 'I didn't know that third drink would go to my head like that.

At least nothing bad happened. It could've been much worse. You could've taken photos of me while I was in my underwear....' She narrowed her gaze at him. 'You didn't, did you?'

His eyebrows slammed together in affront. 'What sort of cad do you think I am?'

She gave a huffy little shrug of her left shoulder. 'Who knows what you might've got up to while I was out of it.' She gave him a beady look and added, 'You took my dress off.'

He did the hair-scrape thing again, and then added to it by dragging the same hand down his face, distorting his handsome features as he let out an exasperated-sounding breath. 'You got the zip jammed. You came out of the bathroom with your dress stuck around your hips. I undid it for you and then you got into bed and went out like a light.'

Lottie tugged at her lip with her teeth. 'I didn't do or say anything embarrassing, did I?'

He cocked one eyebrow in a sardonic arc. 'You mean the bit about wanting to show me how convincing you are at faking an orgasm?'

'I did *not* say that!'

'Sure you did.'

Lottie felt her blush go from her face to her scalp in a hot spreading prickle. 'You're making that up. You're teasing me.' *You'd better be teasing me. The alternative is way too mortifying.*

His dark eyes glinted with malicious enjoyment. 'You also gave a very good impression of being madly in love with me.'

She let out a laugh but it didn't quite make the grade. 'Ha, ha. Very funny. As if I would ever fall in love with someone like you. No one would believe it for a second.'

'Yeah? Well, guess what? The whole world thinks you're in love with me.'

Lottie had forgotten about the rest of the world. Her world had shrunk to the four walls of the Chatsfield Monte Carlo that currently contained her and Lucca. A secret world where she saw facets to his personality no one else saw: his vulnerability when he was sick, his artistic talent, his kindness and concern, his protectiveness, his gallantry. 'Maybe, but they think you're in love with me right on back,' she pointed out. 'I'm the first woman you've spent more than one night with. So far we've spent three nights together. For a playboy that's kind of like being married, isn't it?'

He winced as she said the word. 'Kindly refrain from using that word when in my presence. It makes me want to puke.'

Lottie furrowed her brow. 'What have you got against marriage? I know your parents didn't do such a good job of it, but lots of people manage to live happy and fulfilling lives together. Why not you?'

'Not going to happen.'

'Why not?'

'I'd be bored out of my brain within a week of the ceremony,' he said.

'Not if you married the sort of woman you felt an intellectual equal with,' she said. 'It's no wonder you're bored with the ones you hang around now. They don't know you. They just want to sleep with you for the bragging rights. It's not about who you are as a person. For them it's just sex with a filthy-rich guy who looks hot.'

'Thanks for summing up my sex life so profoundly.'

'You're welcome.'

Lottie didn't see Lucca for most of the day. He'd gone to his suite and presumably showered and shaved and did what men needed to do after spending a night in a chair watching a tipsy girl sleep it off.

But once it got after eight in the evening she began to feel increasingly restless. It didn't seem fair that the world was reading about her smoking-hot fling with the world's most notorious playboy when said playboy was deliberately avoiding her. She decided if they had to be holed up in the Chatsfield Monte Carlo together, then they ought to be… well, *together*, for some of the time at least.

She gave his door a sharp rap. 'Lucca?'

'Go away.'

She frowned at the wood panelling on the door. 'Are you sick again?'

'No.' There was a brief pause where she thought she heard him mutter a curse. 'I'm working.'

'Drawing, you mean? Can I see? Please?' She rattled the doorknob impatiently. 'Let me see. Are you doing the one of me?'

The door opened so quickly Lottie almost fell through the doorway. Lucca towered over her with a brooding scowl on his face. 'Can't you take a hint?'

'Well, pardon me for disturbing the muse or whatever you call it but I'm bored witless in here and I think you should do the honour-able thing and entertain me for a bit since it's your stupid hotel that's locked down because of some ghastly little virus.' Lottie knew she sounded a little petulant, even a little vacu-ous. Knew she was probably giving a very good impersonation of one of his bimbo bed-mates, but the truth was she missed him.

She enjoyed his company. She found it stimulating, exciting. He didn't bow and scrape to her because she was a princess like most men did. He teased her and made her laugh.

And he was so talented and so secretive about it. That intrigued her.

'Can't you watch a movie or something?' he said. 'Read a book? Listen to music? Phone a friend?'

She gave him an arch look. 'I just did, but apparently he's got more important things to do than spend time with me.'

His frown cut deeper into his forehead. 'I'm no friend of yours.'

Lottie brushed past him before he could close the door again, her gaze going to the desk near the window where she could see his art materials set up. 'Oh, you *are* doing the one of me.' She went over and looked at the drawing that he had now started painting. There was a magnifying glass set up and a series of tiny brushes and tubes of paint and a palate where he had mixed some colours. 'It's beautiful. When will it be finished?'

'It won't be unless you get the hell out of here and leave me in peace.'

She turned around to face him. 'Why are you so snarly?'

His expression was tight. Surly. Disgruntled. 'It might've escaped your notice but I didn't get any sleep last night.'

'You looked soundly asleep when I woke up this morning.'

'I have a crick in my neck, thanks to you.'

She pushed her lips out in a mock-sympathetic manner. 'Poor baby. Do you want me to massage it for you?'

He glowered at her. 'Have you been drinking?'

'Why on earth would you think that?' She glared at him in affront. 'Just because I want some company—*your* company, which is not up to much, let me tell you, and I can totally see now why girls only stay half a night with you because you're not very nice—doesn't mean I'm off my face.'

He pointed to the connecting door with a rigidly outstretched arm. 'Out.'

Lottie nudged up her chin. 'You can't order me about. I'm a princess.'

The tight silence ticked like the timing device on a bomb.

Tick.

Tick.

Tick.

He suddenly came at her, swooping her up like a whirlwind in his arms, throwing her over his shoulder and carrying her fireman-style back to her suite. 'Hey! Put me down!' She slapped at his back and his taut behind and kicked her legs up and down but to no avail. He dumped her in an ungainly heap on the middle of her bed.

But she didn't let him have it all his own way.

Somehow she managed to grab a fistful of the front of his shirt, which made him come down with her. The weight of his body landing on top of hers knocked the breath out of her lungs, that and the feel of his pelvis coming into contact with hers.

It was as if the world had stopped.

Froze.

Took stock.

Waited.

Lottie saw the moment he gave in to the pull of desire. She felt it in his body first, the way he swelled and hardened. Then she saw it in his gaze, the way it went to her mouth and stayed there. 'This isn't supposed to happen.' His voice was gravel-rough. '*We're* not supposed to happen.'

Her body was tingling, feverish with excitement, her blood running hot and fast. A little demon was inside her urging her to do and say things she wouldn't normally say or do. And she didn't need the lubricant of a champagne cocktail or two or a lethal vodka chaser to make it easier. She linked her arms around his neck, keeping him close enough to feel his breath mingle with hers. 'Everyone already thinks we're happening so why not let us happen?'

His mouth came to the side of hers, as if he was only allowing himself a taste. He nudged against the fullness of her lips, his breath warm and redolent of mint and good quality coffee and something else that was entirely, irresistibly, unforgettably him.

Lottie shivered as he worked on the other side of her mouth, leaving the main surface area of her lips alone. He tantalised, teased and tortured her with those little tug-and-release nibbles that made her spine tingle like fine grains of sand funnelling through an hourglass.

'I want to be inside you.' His deep voice with its wickedly erotic, incendiary words made her body throb with need and her inner core melt.

'So what's stopping you?'

He nuzzled just below her earlobe, making the sensitive skin leap and dance in excitement. 'You're a good girl.' The point of his raspy tongue sizzled inside the shell of her ear. A teasing flick. In. Out. 'I don't do good girls.'

'I can be bad.' She stroked her tongue over his chin, just below his lower lip, his stubble grazing her like sandpaper. 'I bet I can be *very* bad if you show me how.'

She felt his lips move in a rueful smile against the skin of her neck. 'You might hate me for this in the morning.'

'Why would I do that?' She stroked the side of his jaw. 'This is just a one-night stand, isn't it?'

His eyes meshed with hers in an unreadable lock. 'And you'd be okay with that?'

'Would you?'

He frowned again. 'Sure. One night, it is.'

'Half.' She gave him a deliberately pointed look. 'Come midnight you're out of here and back in your own suite. Agreed?'

Something moved in his gaze, a whip-quick flicker. 'Agreed.' And then his mouth came down on hers.

There was something incredibly exciting about a kiss when you knew it was leading to sex, Lottie thought. The passion of it was that little bit more intense, that little bit more intoxicating. The strokes and thrusts of tongues touching, dancing and mating in that sensual prelude to the main event made her whole body quiver with longing. Desire throbbed through her with an escalating beat, the tempo increasing with every movement of his mouth on hers.

His hands were making short work of her clothes, peeling them from her with a deftness she presumed came from years of practice. But this was no time to be thinking of all the women he had entertained in his bed before.

This was *her* bed and she was entertaining *him*.

It made her feel less conflicted about sleeping with him. She was in control. She was setting down the rules because she couldn't bear to be just another girl he'd slept with. Just another name he forgot before the bed was remade. She wanted him to remember her with clarity. She wanted every moment he spent in her arms to be imprinted on his brain. Every touch of her skin against his, every kiss and caress, every murmur and gasp, she wanted him to remember long after their night of passion was over.

'You taste like chocolate milk,' he said against her lips.

'I raided the minibar.' She kissed him back. Soft. Hard. Soft. 'I always eat chocolate when I'm bored.'

'Then we'd better keep you entertained, hadn't we?'

Lottie shivered as his mouth came down over her breast, sucking on her tight nipple, pulling it into his mouth, taking it gently between his teeth before swirling his tongue over it. She writhed beneath him, frustrated that she was naked except for her knickers and he was still fully clothed. She started working on his shirt, tugging it out of his trousers and peeling it back from his shoulders as her mouth found his. She ran her hands down the strongly corded muscles of his back, dipping below his trousers to feel the taut shape of his buttocks. His erection was hot and probing against her belly, making her need of him all the more intense. An empty ache opened up like a cavern inside her, the pulse of her blood making her breathing laboured.

He left her mouth long enough to heel off his shoes and deal with his trousers. The black underwear went next, revealing him in full arousal. Lottie reached for him, guided by an instinct as old as time, shaping him, stroking him, watching as his face twisted and contorted with pleasure.

'Am I doing it right?'

'Perfect.' He gently pulled her hand away. 'But there'll be time for that later. I have other things to see to first.'

Lottie didn't have time to ask him what things he was referring to. He pressed her back down and showed her with the most intimate caress of all. His mouth and tongue separated her folds, tasting her, touching her ever so gently so she could get used to the contact, waiting for her to give him feedback, none of it verbal. She was too far gone for that. She could only gasp and whimper as wave after wave of pleasure pulsed through her. It was like being picked up by a giant wave, tossed around, rolling, spinning, flying...and then softly coming down to float in the shallows....

She opened her eyes to see Lucca looking at her with a mercurial glint in his gaze. 'You weren't pretending, were you?'

She still felt a little dazed by what her body had experienced. 'That was...out of this world.... I felt like I was shattering into a thousand pieces.'

He stroked a lazy hand down her thigh. 'You're beautiful when you come.'

Lottie wondered why she wasn't feeling awkward or embarrassed. She hadn't given a thought to how she had looked in that most private of moments. All she could think of was how she felt. Her body had experienced the most ecstatic interlude of its entire existence. And he had made her feel that way. 'Thank you…not just for saying that but for doing that….'

'Making you come?'

She tried to keep her tone light and flirty, even though she was experiencing a turn-around of feelings that was as complex as it was unwelcome. 'I can see why women are lining up to get into bed with you. You really are very good at this, aren't you?'

His smile should have looked smug but somehow didn't. He brushed her lower lip with the blunt pad of his thumb, his tone deep with unusual gravitas. 'I don't want to hurt you. If it's been a while you might not be ready for the full deal.'

Lottie stroked her palm against the stubble of his lean cheek. 'I'm ready. I want you. I want to come with you inside me. I want to feel you come.'

He drew in a shuddering breath as if her words had touched on something deeply primal in him. 'I don't think there's any doubt of that happening. I'm only holding on by the width of a hair as it is.'

'Really?' She sounded as surprised as she felt and wondered if she should have toned it down a bit. Was there such a thing as being starstruck by sex? If so, she had just experienced it.

He did that brushlike movement with his thumb on her lower lip again. 'You turned me on the minute I walked into that morning room at the palace and saw you standing there, firing daggers at me from those beautiful green eyes of yours.'

She felt a thrill tingle through her flesh. She had felt it too, that electric tension in the air, the sparks they had struck off each other in enmity.

What sparks would they strike off each other in love?

Love?

The errant concept was a like a splash of cold water. It dripped on her common sense in icy droplets of reality.

Lucca Chatsfield didn't do love. He was only interested in the here and now...as she was. Wasn't she?

Of course she was.

This was a bit of fun—a light-hearted fling to get her back out there. To reclaim what had been taken away from her all those years ago. This was not about finding a life partner, someone to share the joys of life, of having a relationship that was exclusive and full of trust and companionship, of bringing up a family together.

This was about having hot sex with a man she would probably never set eyes on again once her sister's wedding was over.

He tipped up her chin as he searched her gaze for a heartbeat. 'Hey, did I lose you there for a moment?'

Lottie smiled a sultry smile as she brought his head down. 'I'm yours until midnight, remember?'

CHAPTER TEN

LUCCA'S MOUTH MOVED over hers with heart-stopping thoroughness, taking his time with each stroke and glide of his tongue against hers, building her need for him to a point where she was feverish to feel him inside her. Her inner core was slick with a clawing, aching want, a pulse beating so insistently for satiation she moved against him, breathlessly urging him to take things to completion.

He kept her dangling, teasing her to the edge and backing off again, his mouth on her breasts, then underneath them where the skin was baby soft and supersensitive. Then to the cave of her belly button where he swirled his tongue in and out, making her nerves scream for him to go farther down south. His fingers played with her, not enough to set her off but enough to make her desperate for the fulfilment he promised.

She raised her hips off the bed, giving a gasping plea for him to end this torture. 'Now. Please *now*.'

'Condom first.'

Lottie watched as he sheathed himself, held her breath as he came back over her, balancing his weight on his forearms. He took it slowly, far too slowly for her liking, but a part of her secretly delighted in his consideration for her comfort. The shallow sex-crazed hedonist the press painted him as was at complete odds with who was making love to her so tenderly now. Nothing about his movements, his caresses, his kisses, his strokes, had anything selfish about them.

They were all about *her* pleasure. *Her* comfort.

He had put her pleasure before his own. It must be killing him to have to wait so long for his own release. She could feel the turgid length of him against her labia, only his steely self-control delaying the primal urge to mate.

He gently nudged her apart and tested her acceptance of him. 'Tell me if I'm hurting you.' His deep voice was a sexy burr.

'You're not hurting me.' She clutched at his buttocks and drew him in farther. He felt so thick and strong and her body was so wet and greedy for him. She heard him suck in a breath as he went in deeper. She could feel his control wavering. He wanted to bury himself to the hilt but only kindness and consideration for her comfort was stopping him.

Lottie dug her fingers into his taut flesh as she lifted herself up to receive him farther. He glided a little deeper, waiting for her body to accommodate him. Her body gripped him tightly. She felt the ripples of pleasure course through her. Her wetness. His thickness. His strength. Her softness.

She grew more and more impatient. Her body was poised on a precipice. Tense. Titillated. Tortured. Her flesh was crying out. Every nerve screaming, *Now. Now. Now.*

'Please…' Her voice was a gasping plea. 'Oh, please…'

He gave a grunt against her neck as he surged forward, the swollen thickness of him completely filling her, the friction of him delighting her senses, reeling her senses in a crazy whirlpool.

His thrusts were gentle to start with. She could feel him holding himself back in the way he measured each stroke of his body within hers. He gradually increased the rhythm, which felt strangely familiar to her and yet unlike anything she had experienced before. It was as if her body recognised him. Was uniquely tuned to him. Responded to him like no one else. Responded to him with honesty, with naturalness, with enthusiasm and zero self-consciousness.

He slipped a hand between their bodies, caressing her clitoris in soft little teasing strokes that triggered a tumultuous release that reverberated throughout her body, shaking it like the tremors of a powerful earthquake. So intense was her release she momentarily lost all sense of time and space. She was limbless, floating in a languid sea of contentment....

He kept thrusting, working himself to his own release, and taking her along for the ride. She clung to him as his pace quickened, her body tingling at the way his was so thick and tight within hers. She felt the tension building in him, in the strongly defined muscles of his back and shoulders, in his thighs where they were entwined so erotically with her own.

He drew in a breath and let it out in a shuddering whoosh as he emptied himself, the quaking of his body sending aftershocks of pleasure through hers.

Lottie waited for the moment of awkwardness. The messy business of the condom. The furtive scramble for clothes. The regret. The I-shouldn't-have-had-sex-with-you moment that always felt like a blot on her conscience.

It didn't happen.

Instead Lucca brushed a tendril of hair back off her face with a touch as gentle as the sweep of a feather. His expression was not arrogant, proud or smugly satisfied. It was contemplative…thoughtful, searching. 'I didn't hurt you?'

'No…' She touched a fingertip to the small frown that had appeared between his brows, smoothing it like one would do a knotted muscle. 'It was wonderful. You were wonderful.'

He captured her finger and kissed its tip, his eyes holding hers. 'We were wonderful.'

Lottie wasn't naive enough to think he'd found sleeping with her anything out of the ordinary. She had both of her feet firmly planted on the concrete-solid ground of reality. But it was hard to stop a tiny segment of her heart from hoping he had found some-

thing different about their union. Not just her
lack of experience, but her response to him
and his to her. Had he felt that powerful surge
of sensation through his flesh with every
partner he'd ever had? Had he felt the world
spin out of control in that senses-spinning
moment when no thought could anchor itself?

Had he wondered if one night could turn
into many nights?

No.

She put on a breezy smile. 'At least in future I won't have to pretend. My future lovers
will be eternally grateful to you for sorting
that out for me.'

He eased away from her, dealing with the
condom with what seemed unnecessary attention to detail. 'I thought the goal for royally
born girls like you was finding a suitable man
to marry, not go shopping for multiple lovers.'

Lottie rolled onto her stomach and propped
her chin on her crossed-over hands. 'I think
it'd be wise for me to try before I buy. Get a
feel for what I like in a lover. Get a little more
experience. Experiment a bit.'

It was a long moment before he turned to
glance at her over his shoulder. She wondered
if he had paused long enough to assemble

his features into an indifferent expression. 'Go for it.'

She idly kicked her lower legs up and down. 'Maybe you could suggest someone for me. That guy who owned the nightclub seemed—'

'No.' The word was delivered flatly. Implacably. He got up from the bed, snatched his trousers from the floor, stepping into them with what looked like controlled violence.

'What's the matter?'

He picked up his shirt but instead of putting it on he scrunched it in one hand as if it were nothing but yesterday's newspaper. 'Listen to yourself. One orgasm and you're suddenly ready to open your legs for anyone who shows the remotest bit of interest in you?'

'It wasn't one orgasm. It was two.'

He made a sound halfway between a laugh and a muttered curse as he sent his hand through his hair. 'I knew this was going to be a mistake.'

Lottie got off the bed and used the sheet as a wrap around her nakedness. 'I don't know what the fuss is all about. I've a perfect right to express myself sexually with whomever I want. You've had loads of lovers. I've only had two.' She freed her hair from behind the makeshift collar of the sheet. 'I want to make up for all the time I've lost. I'm twenty-three years old and I've only had two orgasms, apart from the ones I—well, let's not go into that. It's not the same thing. It's much nicer with a partner.'

'Make it up with me.'

She looked at him blankly for a moment. 'What?'

'Make the time up with me.' He tossed his balled-up shirt to the wing chair, not even noticing it hit the floor instead. 'Have a relationship with me. Just till your sister's wedding is done and dusted.'

'Did you just say "relationship"?'

'Fling.' A muscle ticked in his jaw. 'I meant a fling.'

She pretended to take her time thinking about it, tapping at her lips with two fingertips. 'I don't know…seems pretty risky to me.'

'Risky?' A frown beetled his brows. 'How?'

'There are a lot of perks to partnering a princess. As social climbing goes you don't get to go much higher.'

His chin jerked backwards. *'Social climbing?'* He let out a swear word in Italian. 'You think that's what this is about?'

She gave him her best arch look. 'What else could it be about?'

He took her by the shoulders in a grip that was undergirded by steel. 'I'll show you,' he said, and crushed his mouth to hers.

Lucca opened his eyes after a long deep sleep and realised he was still in Lottie's bed. She was snuggled up next to him, her cheek resting on his chest, her hair in a sexily mussed-up tangle on the pillow. Her right hand was lying just above his groin. He could already feel the stirring of his blood at the thought of that dainty little hand going lower.

He had never spent the night in anyone's bed but his own. He had never spent the night with anyone, period. But here it was close to 6:00 a.m. and he wanted to drive himself into her hot wet centre and forget about everything but the lust that consumed him when he was with her.

For that's all it was—lust.

He had a strong sex drive. He hadn't had more than a day or two of celibacy since he was a teenager. Which was why this set-up was acceptable for him right now. Even more acceptable since he'd received that email from his father's CEO the day before. He'd almost talked himself into believing that's why he had offered Lottie a fling till the end of the month. *Almost.* The anticipated drop in hotel bookings due to the quarantine imposed in Monte Carlo hadn't occurred elsewhere as expected. Apparently the news of his involvement with Princess Charlotte of Preitalle had precipitated an upswing of bookings in Chatsfield Hotels across the globe, unmatched by any advertising campaign ever conducted before. The romantic mix of prim-and-proper royal and irascible promiscuous rake had somehow lifted the Chatsfield brand to an all-time high.

Lucca felt Lottie stir beside him. One of her feet brushed against his and she gave a little purring murmur as she burrowed closer, her hand closing around him. 'Ooh, is that for me?' she asked.

A shudder of desire shot through him like a lightning bolt. He deftly rolled her beneath him, only pausing long enough to get a condom in place before he entered her in a slick deep thrust. 'Don't tell me you're one of those annoying morning people who insist the day begins at dawn.'

She smiled against his lips. 'You're a fine one to talk. I barely touched you and you sprang to attention.'

He kissed her deeply, stroking her tongue with his, swallowing her gasps and whimpers, pushing her to the edge before backing off. He did it again and again and again, teasing her with the anticipation of release, making her want him so badly she clawed at his back like a cat.

He relished the power he had over her. He needed to prove to himself that she wanted him more than he wanted her. He had never allowed that power balance to shift. He wasn't going to start now. He would have a fling with her but it would be physical, not emotional.

He hooked one of her legs over his hip and drove into her relentlessly, deeper and deeper, faster and faster, until she finally threw her head back and gave a primal scream, her body thrashing and bucking wildly beneath his. Then and only then did he let himself fly free in a shattering orgasm that made his spine buckle as if each vertebra had been loosened.

He rolled off her and lay on his back, taking a moment to get his breathing back under control as the afterglow settled over him like warm, healing rays of sunshine.

Lottie circled one of his nipples with her fingertip. 'Is it always the same for you?'

Lucca kept his eyes closed. 'Not always.'

She sent her finger anticlockwise this time. 'What makes it different?'

You make it different. He pushed the thought away, along with her hand, and got up to dispose of the condom. 'Lots of things.'

'Like what?'

'Energy levels, alcohol consumption, jet lag, mood.' He picked up his trousers, grimaced at the creases and tossed them back on the floor. He turned to see her worrying her bottom lip with her teeth. Something fisted in his chest when he saw the reddened patch of beard rash on her chin. If he had done that to her face what had he done to her with his trying-to-prove-a-point-to-himself lovemaking?

He got his answer when she rose from the bed. She winced as she took her first step but tried to disguise it by turning her back to him as she hunted for her glasses.

'Lottie?' He put a hand on her arm and handed her the frames he had taken off the bridge of her cute little nose the night before. 'Are you sore?'

She put on glasses and a brave smile all at the same time and his gut fisted again. 'I'm fine.'

He gently tipped up her chin. 'You've got beard rash. I'm sorry.' He touched her lower lip with his thumb. 'I should've toned it down a bit.'

'It's fine…I'll put some concealer on it.'

He pressed a soft kiss to the top of her head. 'A warm bath might help. Want me to run you one?'

'That would be lovely.'

A few minutes later Lucca sat on the edge of the Jacuzzi-size bathtub and watched like an indulgent parent as Lottie played with the soap bubbles. 'I can't remember the last time I had a bubble bath,' she said. 'I'd forgotten how much fun it is.' She cupped a handful of bubbles and blew them towards him. 'It'd be more fun if you were in here with me. There's heaps of room. I could practically do laps. Why don't you join me?'

'You know why.' He picked up a handful of bubbles and piled them on her tawny head like a crown.

She gave him a shy little smile and then gathered some more bubbles and placed them on the tops of her bent knees, watching with what seemed studious intent as they wobbled there precariously for a moment before sliding down her legs. 'Do you run bubble baths for your other lovers?'

'No, but I had a hot tub orgy once.'

She made a business of scooping up two more kneepads of bubbles, positioning them just so. 'Was it fun?'

Lucca didn't have to think too long before he answered. 'Not particularly.'

She looked at him then, her gaze direct. 'Why do you use sex as an outlet when you're such a talented artist? Why not put that energy into your drawing and painting instead?'

He got up from the bath's edge and brushed the suds off his thighs. 'You shouldn't stay in too long. You'll get all wrinkly like a prune.'

She turned in the tub to face him, sending bubbles over the edge of the bath like lava flow. 'Why are you running away from your talent? Why are you hiding it from everyone?'

'Talented artists line every street throughout Europe.' He wiped his hands on a towel and stuffed it back on the rail haphazardly. 'Didn't you see some of them the other day outside that restaurant we went to in Nice?'

'Then why aren't you out there with them? At least then other people will get to see your work.'

Lucca resorted to his tried and trusty friend—scorn. 'Oh, yes, I can see that headline. Hotel Chain Heir Touting Amateur Wares on Back Streets of French Riviera. Yeah, that would work.'

'You don't believe you're talented.' She said it as if it were a total shock to her.

It wasn't to him.

He knew his limitations. He knew what it took to get a foothold in the art world.

And it wasn't family money and bedroom charm.

Lucca turned his back on her frowning expression. 'I'm going to see what's happening about this crazy quarantine. The manager was supposed to call me an hour ago to update me.'

'I'll pose for you.'

He stopped at the bathroom door and turned to look at her. She was standing in a sea of bubbles, her hands cupped across her breasts and her feminine mound like a modern-day version of Sandro Botticelli's *Birth of Venus*.

His breath snagged in his throat like a fine cotton shirtsleeve catching on a nail. She was all that he was not: innocence and beauty. Trust and honesty. Decency and integrity. Sweetness and sincerity.

Her gaze challenged his in a little lock that made her eyes look like green sea glass. 'I want you to draw me, Lucca.'

'I've drawn you.'

'Not like that.' Her hands fell from her body to hang by her sides. 'Like this.'

Lucca let his gaze soak up the sight of her. She had never looked more beautiful than she did right now. How could he not want to draw her? To capture this moment when her body told him a story that only he and she knew. A private sensual tale of two opposites finding something in the other that no one else could ever understand. He didn't understand it himself. It was a story he was still uncovering. Page by page. Chapter by chapter. Scene by scene. Word by word.

Discovering layers to her and of himself he had not realised were there until now. 'Why?'

'Because I want to see how you see me.'

'I've never done a nude before.' He gave her a flash of his bad-boy smile. 'Well, not like that, I mean.'

'That will make it even more special. Something that's just between us. No one else has to see it. I wouldn't want anyone else to see it. It'll be totally private.'

He rubbed a hand over the back of his head, still wrestling with his conscience. It was a surprise to him that he still had one. A big surprise. He saw the trust shining in her bright clear gaze and felt like something dark and dirty inside him had been cleansed. 'I thought you said art was to be shared?'

'It will be shared.' Her dimples appeared as she smiled. 'By us.'

'Can I look now?' Lottie asked the following afternoon.

'No, sit still while I get the angle of the light falling across your shoulder.'

'But I'm getting cold.'

'Hey, sweetheart, this was your idea, remember?' He dipped his paintbrush and bent back to the task, his concentration fiercely played out on his features, making him look formidable and cross rather than playboy handsome.

Lottie wasn't cold so much as she was dying to see what he had done. They were due to fly back to the island tomorrow now the quarantine had been lifted. The bug had been identified as food poisoning, ironically from a bakery that supplied the hotel. Only a handful of guests had been affected but the authorities had taken conservative measures to keep the infection contained.

The time spent with Lucca had more than made up for any inconvenience. She could not remember a time when she'd felt as happy and contented in someone's presence. The private Lucca was not the public Lucca, or maybe she brought out a different side to him. She didn't delude herself with the thought their relationship—*fling*—would last longer than it took for Madeleine and Edward to drive out of the Chatsfield Hotel driveway with Just Married written in shaving foam on the back windscreen.

But at least she would have something of him to keep with her always. His painting of her would be a reminder of the first time in his life when he had committed to something—*someone*—for more than a few hours.

'Right.' He sat back and wiped his forehead with a paint-smeared cloth that looked suspiciously like a Chatsfield Hotel hand towel. 'It needs a few more touches but I'll do that when we get back. This coat has to dry before I add any more detail.'

Lottie stepped out of the bath and quickly dried her feet and ankles on a towel before coming to look over his shoulder. 'Do I really look like that?'

He frowned. 'What? You don't like it?'

She suddenly realised he was uncertain and hiding it behind a gruff impatience. 'I don't know... ' She put a finger to her lips and tapped against them as if in deep critical thought. 'I think you could've done a better job with my breasts.'

'What do you mean?' He scowled at her irritably. 'I spent bloody ages on your breasts. They're perfect. They've got just the right amount of form and light and shadow.'

Lottie tapped him on the end of his nose

with a playful fingertip, flashing him a cheeky got-you smile. 'You are such a sensitive boy.'

'Little witch.' He grabbed her by the hips and pulled her close, taking her right breast into the hot cavern of his mouth and drawing deeply.

She looked down at his dark head against her white skin and shivered. She stroked her fingers through his closely cropped hair, breathing in the scent of the signature Chatsfield shampoo. She wondered with a sharp little pang if there would be a time in the future when she could smell cedarwood, leather, white rose and lavender and not think of him.

Lucca's mouth went to her other breast, his tongue teasing the nipple into a hardened point. Her belly turned over in delight as one of his hands left her hip to cup her intimately. She pushed against him, wanting more, aching for him with every throbbing cell of her being.

'We're supposed to be giving you a rest,' he said.

'I'm rested.'

'No, you're not.' He put her from him but softened it with a rueful smile. 'Stop tempting me, baby girl. Don't you know creative types are easily distracted?'

'I like distracting you.' She traced his bottom lip with her finger, then over his top one. 'You look so intense when you're working. You get deep frown lines here.' She touched his forehead. 'You look moody and grumpy, sort of like Beethoven.'

He gave a self-deprecating laugh. 'Yes, well, that's a side of me no one else sees. Thank God.'

Lottie put her hands on his shoulders and looked into dark brown eyes. 'You're a good person, Lucca Chatsfield. Don't let anyone ever tell you any different.'

'Don't go pinning any angel wings on me, little princess.' His eyes contained a dangerous glint. 'I'm rotten to the core.'

'I don't believe that.'

His hands cupped her bottom, bringing her between his spread thighs. His erection was tenting his jeans; she could feel it pressing against her thigh, making her need of him all the more desperate. She reached down and undid his waistband, sliding his zip down and freeing him to her hand, caressing that proudly jutting flesh as she watched pleasure play out over his features. 'You like it when I do that?'

'What do you think?'

She rubbed his shaft up and down, rolling her fingertip over the bead of moisture that oozed from his tip. 'I want to pleasure you.'

'Here's the thing.' He stood and scooped her up in his arms. 'I have this little rule about ladies coming first. Call me old-fashioned but that's the way I always do things.'

Lottie quivered with anticipation as he lowered her to the bed in his suite. His eyes were black with desire as he parted her legs, stroking the sensitive skin of her inner thighs, ramping up her excitement with each slow caress. By the time he put his mouth to her she was already flying. Her back arched off the bed, her fingers clawing at the bedcover as wave after wave of ecstasy rippled through her. The intensity of her response to him always shocked her. It took her by surprise each and every time. Her response was never quite the same. There were new things to learn about her body each time he touched her.

But now it was time for her to learn more about his.

Lottie pushed him onto his back on the bed

and straddled him. He was fully engorged, painfully so if the look on his face was anything to go by. 'I want to suck you dry.' She could barely believe she had said the shockingly erotic words, let alone meant them.

'Not without a condom.'

'Why not?'

'Because it's safer for you with one.' He reached for protection in the bedside drawer and handed it to her. 'You can put it on me if you like.'

She took it from him and tore the packet with her teeth. 'Can I put it on with my mouth?'

'You're inner bad girl is letting it all hang out tonight, isn't she?'

She gave him a teasing look. 'Do you think you can you handle her?'

He smiled a wickedly sexy smile. 'Let's see, shall we?'

CHAPTER ELEVEN

THE PRESS WERE waiting for them as they landed in Preitalle the following day but for once in her life Lottie didn't shy away from the surge of people and the flash of cameras. Her body was still humming from Lucca's passionate lovemaking the night before, not to mention a quick hot interlude in the shower before they left the hotel that morning. It was a new experience to be the darling of the press and she lapped it up while Lucca led her to the waiting car. He handled all the questions with his usual charm and good humour, even the question about a second royal wedding.

'Let's get the first one out of the way first,' he said with an easy smile.

Madeleine, however, was not so happy about the way the press had taken to Lottie's affair with Lucca, and took her aside once he had left for the hotel. 'Do you realise what you're doing?' she said.

'I'm going out and having a life just like you told me to.'

'Your affair with Lucca Chatsfield is taking the attention off my wedding.' Madeleine scowled. 'Not one camera looked my way when we were out there just then. No one even spoke to me. They were all clicking away at you and him as if it were you two getting married and not me and Edward.'

'It was your idea to bring him here,' Lottie reminded her.

'He's supposed to be helping you with the wedding.'

'He *is* helping me with the wedding. He's in charge of the hens' night. It's going to be fun. Just you wait and see.'

Madeleine was still scowling as she followed Lottie to her office. 'You're not really in love with him, are you?'

Lottie put her mobile phone on the desk next to her computer. Lucca had been sending her smoulderingly hot texts to remind her of what he was going to do to her when he finally got her alone. Her body reacted to each one as if he had reached through the phone and touched her. She clicked off the screen so her sister couldn't see his latest missive. 'No, of course not, but I do like him. He's fun to be around. He makes me laugh.'

Madeleine humphed. 'He's not in love with you even if he acts as if he is. He's just using you to fill in the time before he collects his allowance.'

Lottie felt a sharp little pain near the bottom of her heart as if something was trying to tug it down below her rib cage. She knew Lucca's motives were not entirely pure. She knew he was only here for his family's money and that he would not let anything or anyone stop him from collecting what he felt he was entitled to, but she hated being reminded of it, especially by her sister, who had found a man who loved her so completely and unreservedly. 'I know what I'm doing.'

'I don't want anything to spoil my wedding.' Madeleine pressed her lips together for a moment. 'You almost ruined my twenty-first birthday with your silly little fling with that diplomat's son. I hope you're not going to let history repeat itself.'

Lottie jolted as if her sister had slapped her. What about what had happened to *her*? What about *her* devastation at being exploited? At being exposed in such a degrading way? 'If you're so worried I'm going to stuff everything up for you, then why did you ask me to be your wedding planner?'

'Because I felt sorry for you.'

The words fell into the room like a hand grenade.

Lottie swallowed a painful lump in her throat. *Pity*. The one thing she hated more than anything else. 'Is that why you agreed to have Lucca Chatsfield come over here to spice up my woefully pathetic social life?'

A hard look came into her sister's eyes. 'Have a fling with him but try and keep it out of the headlines, okay? This is the most important day of my life. I don't want anyone on centre stage but me.'

Lucca knew Lottie was upset as soon as she stepped into the Chatsfield bar where he had arranged to meet her. She didn't show it on her face. It was the way she carried herself. Stiffly. As if she was carrying an invisible weight on her head that at any moment was going to topple off. He pulled out a chair for her. 'You look like you need a couple of champagne cocktails to loosen up.'

Her eyes seemed to be having trouble meeting his. 'Sorry I'm late.'

'Two minutes isn't late.' He gently flicked her cheek with his finger. 'I guess it is when you're a control freak, huh?'

She gave him a tight smile before looking away again. 'My sister's upset with me.'

He brought her chin back round so she met his gaze. 'What? She didn't like the lingerie?'

Her forehead was puckered with a frown. 'She doesn't like the fact that our fling is taking the attention off her.'

Lucca felt his stomach stumble like a foot misjudging a step. Did she want to end their relationship ahead of schedule? The thought was disturbingly uncomfortable. *Unfamiliar.* What did he care if she ended it? There were plenty of women who would willingly take her place in his bed. He could replace her in a heartbeat. 'Aren't you entitled to your share of the limelight?'

She let out a breath that made her shoulders slump. 'I can't seem to please her. For years she's been at me to get out more. Now I'm finally out having a bit of fun and she wants me to tone it down.'

'Ever thought of telling her to mind her own business?'

She gave him a fleeting smile. 'I'd have to have a vodka chaser or two first.'

'Why are you afraid of standing up to her?'

She slowly traced the C on the Chatsfield coaster on the bar in front of her. 'I don't know…I guess it's because she's never put a foot wrong. She never makes a blunder.' She pushed the coaster away as if it had suddenly annoyed her and looked at him. 'Is must be wonderful to go through life without ever making a mistake.'

Lucca didn't like to think too closely about some of the mistakes he'd made. There were too many of them to think about. They were backed up behind him like a row of wrecked and abandoned cars, going all the way back to his childhood. He brushed his knuckles beneath her chin. 'Want to go somewhere a little more private?'

Her eyes got that sparkle in them that always made his groin tighten. 'Where did you have in mind?'

He took her hand and pulled her to her feet. 'I have an etching to show you.'

Lottie held the painting Lucca had done of her in her hands. It was no bigger than a post-card even with the frame he'd organised for it. 'It's beautiful....' She traced the gilt edge of the frame with her fingertip. 'I don't think I've ever been given anything more beauti-ful.' She swivelled to look at him. 'Thank you.'

He gave one of his indifferent shrugs. 'Count yourself lucky. You're the first lover I've ever given a gift to.'

She put the painting down on the dressing table, watching him covertly in the mirror. 'What will you do with the one of me in the palace gardens?'

'File it away somewhere, I suppose.'

'I think you should show it to a top gallery owner in London or New York. Set up a solo exhibition. It would be a way to launch your career as an artist. Painting a royal portrait is every artist's—'

'No.'

She wrinkled her brow. 'But why? What's the point of doing such delicate and exquisite work and hiding it in the bottom drawer as if you're ashamed of it?'

His expression tightened. 'My artwork is private. I want to keep it that way.'

'But why?'

'Because there's nothing else in my life that *is* private.'

Lottie looked at him oddly. 'But I thought you liked drawing all that attention to yourself. You seem to deliberately court scandal. You said it's your brand.'

He pushed a hand through his hair. 'Leave it, *cara*. I'm not after a big career in the arts.'

'What *do* you want, Lucca?'

His eyes moved away from hers. 'You know what I want. I want my share of the family trust fund.'

She rose from the dressing-table stool and came over to him. 'You've had money all your life and it hasn't made you happy.'

'What makes you think I'm not happy?'

Lottie looked into his masked gaze. 'Happy people don't create negative drama, even if it's mostly directed at themselves.'

A mocking smile tilted his mouth. 'You should ask for a refund on that psychoanalyst degree you're brandishing about. It's rubbish.'

'That's a defence mechanism of yours. You make a joke of everything but inside you're not laughing. You're hurting.'

A line of tension rippled through his jaw but his smile was all easy laid-back charm. 'Listen, sweetheart, we have two weeks to get through before your sister's wedding. The world is kind of hooked on us getting it on so calling it quits right now would upset a lot of people and take the shine off your sister's big day. Not to mention ruin my chances of claiming my trust fund. But hey, I'll give you the choice. I'm cool either way.'

Lottie rolled her lips together. Did he really not give a damn whether their relationship continued or not? How could he be so easy going about it? Had she made no impression on him at all? Did he care nothing for her other than as just another lover he had taken to his bed?

It would serve him right if she did end it. But of course she wouldn't. *Couldn't.*

Madeleine had already cautioned her about overshadowing her big day. Ending her affair with Lucca would draw a lot of unnecessary attention.

Besides, she didn't want it to end.

Her heart gave a painfully tight squeeze. Admitting her feelings was dangerous. It made her want to think about things she had no business thinking about…Lucca and her together, not just for a couple of weeks but for a lifetime. Getting married. Having babies. Building a life of happiness and security for their family that he had missed out on in his lonely and traumatic childhood. Pipe dreams…all of them. That was the trouble with falling in love with a man who didn't believe in love lasting. How many women thought they were the one to unlock a closed heart only to have theirs broken for their effort? Thousands. Millions.

'I don't want anything to spoil Madeleine and Edward's wedding,' she said.

He gave a slow nod. 'Fine.'

There was a moment of silence.

'You wouldn't really forfeit your trust fund…would you?'

'Not for the sake of two weeks.'

What about for the sake of me? Lottie pushed the thought aside before it could get a foothold. 'Is it a lot of money?'

He picked up her royal-crested silver hairbrush and turned it over in his hands. 'Not by some people's standards.'

'But it's what it represents, right?'

He stood behind her and started brushing her hair. Long, deliciously sensual strokes that made each hair on her head shiver in ecstasy. 'I know you think I'm a blood-sucking parasite but—'

'*Please* don't remind me of how outspoken I was that day.'

He smiled at her crookedly in the mirror but it was another one of those sad smiles that made her heart constrict at the thought of the pain and loneliness he had experienced as a child. 'Has anyone ever told you what beautiful hair you have?'

He was changing the subject, another defence mechanism he had perfected. But this time she didn't call him on it. He had his reasons for wanting to claim his family's money. It was no business of hers to criticise him for it or to try and dissuade him from following through on it. 'You did…last night.'

'So I did.' He turned her so she was facing him. He tilted up her face and looked into her gaze for endless seconds, his thumb moving back and forth over her cheek like a slow-beating arm of a metronome. 'It's true, little princess. You are beautiful.'

Lottie put her hand over his. 'I've never felt it until I met you.'

He slid his hand out from under hers and used it to tuck her hair back behind her ear as if she was six years old. 'I have to get back to the hotel. There's a staff issue my father's CEO wants me to look into.' Was it her imagination or had his voice sounded deeper and huskier than normal?

He was at the door before she could find her own voice and it too came out husky. 'Lucca?'

He glanced at her over his shoulder. 'Yes?'

'Thank you…'

'For?'

'Just…thank you.'

His hand fell away from the doorknob as a frown settled on his forehead. 'Lottie…you do realise this thing we've got going is not going to continue once I leave here, don't you?'

Lottie fought hard to keep her expression serenely composed. 'But of course. How could it? I live here. You live in England. Long-distance relationships never work. And I hate flying, remember?'

He gave another slow nod. 'Good. Glad we got that sorted.'

'You're not having second thoughts, are you?'

'Good God, no.' His laugh was like a punch to her heart. 'I'm surprised I've lasted this long.'

'Not bored out of your brain yet?'

There was something about his smile that wasn't quite right. It looked tight. Fixed. 'Surprisingly, no. You?'

She rocked her hand back and forth. 'So-so.'

His frown deepened and then it suddenly relaxed as he laughed again. 'Little minx.' He came back over and scooped her up in his arms and carried her towards the bed.

'What about the terribly important staff issue at the hotel?' Lottie asked.

He dropped her on the mattress and came

down over her, pinning her with his weight, his eyes glinting at her darkly. 'There's something far more urgent I have to see to here first.'

CHAPTER TWELVE

THE MORNING OF the wedding dawned bright and sunny after almost two weeks of inclement weather. Lottie had listened patiently each day as Madeleine fussed and fretted about how her hair would be a disaster and her make-up would run and how the guests wouldn't be able to see her for all the umbrellas, blah, blah, blah.

Privately she thought her sister was turning into a Bridezilla but of course she didn't say anything. It was a big event in Madeleine's life and as a royal princess and heir to the throne it was an even bigger pressure to have everything run according to plan.

Lottie had kept her relationship with Lucca out of the spotlight out of respect for Madeleine and Edward's wedding. But rather than diminish the intensity of their relationship it had fuelled it. Meeting in secret, stealing moments or half-hours without anyone noticing, had given their relationship an even more exciting edge.

They had worked as a team to fine-tune the last details of the ceremony and reception. Lucca might not have been to a wedding before but he was fabulous at getting people to do what he wanted. He issued orders with such charm he had every palace and hotel staff member working overtime to please him.

Everyone was still talking about the spectacular success of the hens' night. Even Lottie had enjoyed herself dressing up and dancing till the wee hours, especially as Lucca had sneaked in disguised as one of the waiters and stolen a steamy kiss behind one of the DJ's subwoofers.

But even if they had not mentioned it again, Lottie was all too well aware that three days after the wedding their relationship would draw to a close. By staying the month Lucca would have fulfilled the terms of the arrangement made by his father's CEO. His trust fund would be secure and he would go back to London to his life of living in the fast lane at supersonic speed.

Lottie had cleverly compartmentalised her brain. When she was with Lucca she was totally in the moment, pretending they were a proper couple with the potential for a future together. It was only when she was alone that the other side of her brain took over, leaving her unusually teary and agitated until she could barely sleep.

She hadn't meant to fall in love with him. She hadn't meant to even like him. But somehow over the past couple of weeks she had grown to know him as a person. Not the laugh-a-minute layabout lad-about-town image he projected, but the sensitive and artistic man who had greater depth to his character than he let on.

Knowing him on that level made her heart open like an orchid does to tropical sunshine. How had she ever thought love was something she could control? It had sneaked up on her, catching her unawares, dismantling her defences in a sensual ambush that made her body ache to be with him every minute she could. Every moment she spent with him made her love for him grow stronger. She felt her heart squeeze every time he smiled at her. When his eyes gave her that wickedly dark glint she melted. Would she be able to carry the pretence to that final goodbye, waving him off as if she felt nothing more for him than a mild affection?

However, if Lucca was suffering any apprehension about their imminent break-up he showed no sign of it. He was his usual affable playful self, making her laugh and teasing her with his usual good humour and filling their private moments with spine-tingling passion that made her body shudder and quake with pleasure.

Once the hair and make-up team had finished with the bridal party, Lottie took a moment to speak to Madeleine as she helped her with her veil. 'You look amazing. Edward is going to be absolutely speechless when he sees you.'

Madeleine placed a hand on her stomach, her expression tight with panic. 'I feel sick with nerves. I keep thinking something is going to go wrong. I'm going to trip in these heels or the back of my dress is going to split while the whole world is watching. Do you think I look fat? Oh, God, what if everyone thinks I'm fat?'

Lottie squeezed her sister's trembling hands. 'You look stunning. Just as a princess should look.'

Madeleine bit her lip. 'Oops, can't do that. I'll ruin my lipstick. Have I got it on my teeth?' She bared her teeth for Lottie to inspect.

'No. You're fine.'

'I can't believe this is my wedding day.' Madeleine's eyes shimmered with tears. 'I'm so happy, Lottie. I wish you could find someone as nice as Edward. I know you think he's boring but he's such a sweetheart. So kind and thoughtful and loving.'

'I didn't say he was boring.' Lottie carefully avoided her sister's gaze as she straightened out a kink in the metres-long veil.

'I know he's nothing like Lucca Chatsfield.' Madeleine smoothed her hands over her hips as she inspected her image in the floor-to-ceiling mirror. 'But at least he's in for the long haul. You do realise Lucca's going to scoot back to London as soon as he's pocketed his trust fund, don't you?'

Lottie tried to ignore the stab of pain her sister's comment evoked. 'I've always known where I stood with him.'

Madeleine toyed with the heirloom diamonds and pearl necklace around her neck, catching Lottie's gaze in the mirror. 'Look, I'm sorry I was a bit of a cow when you got back from Monte Carlo....'

'It's fine.' Lottie pretended to have an interest in the way the neckline of her bridesmaid dress was draping. 'The press have pretty much lost interest. Your wedding is what everyone wants to hear about now and that's as it should be.'

Madeleine's hand fell away from her jewellery as she gave Lottie a probing look. 'You haven't fallen in love with him, have you?'

Lottie kept her expression masked. 'What on earth gives you that idea?'

'He's very attractive.'

'So?'

'So be careful, that's all I'm saying.' Madeleine went back to inspecting her image. 'Men like Lucca Chatsfield don't fall in love with girls like you.'

Resentment weighted Lottie's stomach like an anchor. 'What's wrong with me?'

'You're not his type.'

'How do you know his type?' Lottie said. 'You don't know him. You only know what you've read in the press about him. You haven't spent hours in his company when no one else was around. You don't know how intelligent he is. How kind he is. How incredibly talented he is. You don't know him at all.'

Madeleine raised her brows sceptically. 'Talented at what? Sex? Creating shocking scandals that cause enormous embarrassment to his family? Come on, Lottie. You're letting your fling with him distort your judgement. He's not good at anything other than showing a girl a good time.'

Lottie pressed her lips together. His art was the one thing Lucca said he wanted to keep private. She would honour that. 'We should get moving. The photographer wants some more shots before we leave for the cathedral.'

Lucca had considered giving the wedding a miss but changed his mind at the last minute. He knew Lottie would be feeling nervous that everything would run according to plan. Her role as maid of honour would be adding another layer of pressure on her so he figured he would keep an eye on things in the background so she could concentrate on her duties. It didn't have anything to do with making the most of his last moments with her. He was all set to head back to London once the month was officially over. That was the deal and he was sticking to it. Once his money was secured he'd be gone.

Just three more days and he would have what he wanted.

A huge crowd of people and paparazzi had gathered outside the cathedral but he'd been expecting that. He already had his jokes and one-liners ready for any speculation about his attendance at an event he so far had managed to avoid.

'Lucca Chatsfield.' A journalist pressed through the crowd to thrust a microphone at him. 'Social media is going wild with a nude portrait of Princess Charlotte. There's some speculation going around that you're the artist. Do you have a comment to make?'

Lucca felt his guts turned to gravy. How on earth had that leaked out? And today of all days. Lottie would be devastated. Humiliated by him. Betrayed by him. *Tainted by him.*

Another journalist surged towards him

and another and another until he was backed against the cold stone of the cathedral.

'An art critic in London has said the portrait is the work of a master. What do you say to that, Lucca?'

The questions kept firing at him like poisoned darts.

'How long have you been painting?'

'Have you got an exhibition planned?'

'What's the asking price on the princess's portrait?'

'Someone's offering to pay three million pounds for it. Will you take it?'

Lucca shoved the microphones away with a savage thrust of his hand. 'Get out of my way.'

'Does the princess know you've shared her portrait with the world?'

'Here's the bridal party coming now,' one of the photographers said.

Lucca's stomach plummeted when the paparazzi turned as a whole towards the royal cavalcade. Four black-and-gold carriages drawn by snow-white horses came clip-clopping towards the cathedral as a volley of trumpets sounded. Lottie was in the first carriage with three other bridesmaids looking more beautiful than he had ever seen her. Her world was about to be shattered and there was no way of protecting her, of even warning her before the press surged on her like hyenas on an unsuspecting fawn.

He had never felt more disgusted with himself. He had brought this on her. Not only had he ruined everything for her, he had ruined her sister's wedding day. The event Lottie had worked so hard at making as perfect as she possibly could.

He had destroyed it.

He had destroyed her reputation. Smeared it. Soiled it.

He had destroyed any iota of respect she had gained for him over the past three and half weeks. From now on she would look at him with disgust and loathing. She would hate him when he had hoped...what had he hoped?

He couldn't—wouldn't—allow himself to think of what he had hoped. Hope wasn't a currency he used. He was a playboy—a hardened cynical playboy who didn't believe in hope and love and commitment.

Lucca saw the moment she found out. He watched in powerless misery as her world

came crashing down. He thought he was
going to be physically ill. He felt the sour
bile come up in his throat as her face paled
as a journalist held up a smartphone screen
to the window of the carriage as it passed by.

She would immediately blame him for
leaking it even though he had shown no one.
Not a living soul. He hadn't even taken a picture of it. It had been his gift to her. He had
given her a part of himself. A part he had
given no one else.

Lucca turned away rather than have her
seek his face out in the crowd and look at
him with searing hatred and disgust. He
wouldn't stay to do any more damage to her
or to her family. The only option was to distance himself as soon as he could and hope
the scandal would leave the island with him.

'How could you do this to me?' Madeleine
said sotto voce to Lottie as they assem-
bled out the front of the cathedral. 'First my
twenty-first and now my wedding. What
were you thinking?'

Lottie was still reeling from seeing her
portrait flashing up on what seemed like a
thousand phone screens. How could she stop

the scandal from snowballing? It was like a runaway train storming right through the centre of her sister's wedding day, smashing everything in its way.

But through all the hysteria and mayhem there was a quiet calm place inside her that was certain of one thing—Lucca hadn't leaked that portrait to the press.

'There's nothing to make a fuss about. Keep calm. Keep smiling. Show them nothing is going to spoil your special day.'

Madeleine was close to tears. 'Did you do it deliberately? You've always been jealous of me. Is that why you did it on the most important day of my life?'

'I didn't do it,' Lottie said. 'And neither did Lucca.'

Madeleine gave a choked sound that skirted on the edge of hysteria. 'Oh, you stupid girl, of course he did. Why else did he have a fling with you? He wanted a scandal and now he's got one and it's ruined my wedding day.'

'It hasn't ruined anything.' Lottie was surprised at how calm and in control she felt now the first shock had passed. What did it matter if her naked body was all over the press? She was proud of how Lucca had painted her. It was a beautiful portrait, an intimate one but not an exploitative one. He had captured her at full maturity, with full consent, not furtively behind her back to laugh about with his friends. It had been his gift to her. He had given her a piece of himself she would always treasure.

But before she could talk to Lucca she had to get her sister up that aisle as planned. She took Madeleine's arm and led her back to their father, who was waiting patiently to escort his eldest daughter to the altar. 'We're going to walk tall into the cathedral and you're going to concentrate on focusing your attention on Edward.'

'Your naked body is going to be all over the press instead of my wedding photos!'

'You look so stunning that even if every bridesmaid and groomsman and the entire congregation stripped naked right here and now no one would notice,' Lottie said. 'If you react the way the press want you to it will blow out of all proportion. This is *your* day. Nothing or no one can spoil it unless you let them. Now, let's get a move on. We're already forty minutes behind schedule. Poor Edward will think you've jilted him.'

Madeleine took a deep shuddering breath. 'I suppose you're right. It's just…why now? Why not a few days ago when we could've done something to hush it up?'

Lottie gave her sister's white-gloved hand a squeeze. 'That's not how the world works. Smile, *chérie*. This is your moment. Own it.'

The wedding ceremony went ahead but the whole time Lottie kept wondering where Lucca was. She couldn't see him in the crowd, but then she wasn't wearing her glasses because she hadn't wanted to wreck the wedding photographs, so if he was more than a few feet away she wouldn't know one way or the other. She wanted him to be here to see the result of their combined effort. He had helped her in so many little ways, suggesting touches she hadn't thought of, giving the event a thoroughly modern feel that perfectly complemented the traditional aspects of a royal wedding.

During the signing of the register Lottie turned to one of the groomsmen she had seen Lucca talking to at the rehearsal the day before. Apparently they had met at Cambridge a few months before Lucca had been expelled. 'Adam, have you seen Lucca about? I can't see him anywhere in the congregation.'

'I sent him a text before the ceremony when you guys were so late getting here,' Adam said. 'He sent a text back to say he was leaving.'

Lottie's heart lurched. 'Leaving? What, you mean leaving the island?'

'Apparently.'

She swallowed a golf ball of dismay. How could he leave? He would forfeit his trust fund if he left before the month was up. He couldn't leave. Surely he *wouldn't* leave?

She glanced at her bracelet watch. The signing of the register would take another fifteen minutes at least given the size of the bridal party. Then there were the official photographs back at the palace, which would take an hour and a half, two if Madeleine had one of her fuss fests about her make-up or hair. Lucca would be long gone if Lottie didn't intercept him. Was he leaving because of the portrait? But why? Surely he'd just laugh it off....

Lottie handed Adam her bridesmaid bouquet as well as the bridal one she'd been in charge of while Madeleine signed the wedding certificate. 'Can you hold these for me for a couple of minutes? I have to check on something.'

Adam took the bouquets with a worried grimace. 'This doesn't mean I'm next in line to get married, does it?'

Lucca closed the lid of his leather case and zipped the catch. His heart felt so heavy it dragged at his insides as if a blacksmith's anvil was tied to it. He had never meant to hurt Lottie. He never meant to hurt anyone but somehow it was what he did best. He was the High Priest of Hurting People. If he stayed in someone's life long enough they got hurt.

Lottie was his latest victim. Her reputation would be beyond redemption after this. Her fling with him would go down in history as the scandal that ruined her sister's wedding day. The wedding day Lottie had planned with such meticulous detail. There was no way he could make it up to her. Apologising was a waste of time. She would never believe he hadn't leaked that portrait to the press. He didn't even know whom to blame…other than himself. He had unwittingly exposed her to ridicule. To a scandal that trumped everything he had done in the past.

The knock at the door reminded him he had a car waiting to take him to the ferry port. He had decided against a helicopter. It would make too much noise while the wedding festivities were going on and draw even more attention. He opened the door and blinked in shock. 'Lottie?'

'I had to see you.'

He frowned. 'What are you doing here?'

'That's what I'm here to ask you.' She marched into the room and turned and faced him. 'Adam Brightman told me you're leaving.'

He left the door open. She wouldn't be staying long. She was only here to flay him alive. Might as well get it over with. He deserved it. He scraped a hand through his hair. 'I think I've done enough damage around here without hanging around to witness the fallout.'

She stood looking at him with her shiny bright green eyes, which looked naked without her frames. She'd told him she hadn't wanted to spoil her sister's wedding photographs with wearing glasses even though she couldn't see more than a metre in front of her without them and couldn't tolerate contacts. It was yet another example of how she always put others before herself. 'I know you didn't leak the portrait to the press.'

Lucca's frowned deepened. 'You do?'

Her expression was so earnest, so young and fresh. So beautiful...*so decent*. 'I know you, Lucca. You might like a laugh and mock anyone who takes life too seriously but you would never deliberately hurt someone you care about.'

'You think I care about you?' Somehow his mocking tone had lost its edge.

She kept looking at him in that honest direct way that made his chest feel warm, as if a single ray of sunshine had found its way to the cold hard marble of his heart. 'You care more about me than you do your trust fund, otherwise you wouldn't be leaving.'

He gave a careless shrug. 'I don't want my family's money.' He waited a beat and added, 'I got an offer on your portrait. Three million pounds. Not bad for an amateur, huh?'

'You won't sell it. Anyway, you can't. I still have it and I'm not giving it back.'

Lucca kept his expression masked. 'Do you have any idea of who leaked it to the press?'

'I don't know...probably one of the house-maids. I usually keep it in my drawer but a couple of days ago I left it on the dressing table while I went with Madeleine to her dress fitting. All it would take is a quick photo with a smartphone and the rest is history.'

'Is your sister mad?'

'She was at first, but she's forgotten all about it now the press are saying she's the most beautiful bride since Princess Grace of Monaco.' She gave him a self-effacing smile. 'A tiny sketch of me in the bath, no matter how brilliantly painted it is, is never going to outshine her.'

'I'm sorry.' He scraped his hand through his hair again. 'God, what a mess I make of things. I only have to look at someone and I hurt them.'

She came over to him and laid a gentle hand on his arm. 'Lucca, please don't leave until after the wedding. Stay the full time. Please?'

He removed her hand and put some distance between them, standing with his back to her as he looked at the view from the penthouse window. 'It's not about the money.' He watched as the ferry he was booked to leave on motored its way across the ocean towards the Preitalle dock. 'No amount of money is ever going to make up for growing up without a mother or for having a father who prefers the company of a bottle rather than his children.'

He turned and looked at her again. 'Three and a half weeks ago all I could think about was how I was going to get my hands on that trust fund. But now...' He swallowed as an unexpected lump came up in his throat. He couldn't remember the last time he had felt strangled by emotion. 'Your trust...the way you came in here and told me you knew I hadn't betrayed you meant far more to me than any amount of money.'

Her eyes began to shimmer. 'Do you really mean that?'

He came to her and took both of her hands in his. How he loved the feel of her skin against his, the way her small hands fit so completely in his as if seeking his protection.

'I've never met anyone who's as beautiful on the inside as she is on the outside.'

Another self-deprecating smile twisted her mouth. 'Flatterer.'

'I'm serious, *cara*.' He gave her hands a gentle squeeze. 'You're the most beautiful person I could ever wish to spend my life with.'

Her eyes rounded. Blinked. He even heard her gulp. 'Did you say your…*life*?'

Lucca pulled her closer. 'I'm asking you to marry me.'

Her mouth fell open. 'How many vodka chasers have you had?'

He chuckled at her incredulous expression. 'Am I so rubbish at this that you don't believe me? I'm trying to tell you I love you.'

'How can you possibly love *me*?'

'How can I possibly not? I think I fell in love with you the first moment I met you.' He cupped her face in his hands. 'It's taken me till now to realise it. You make me a better person. I *feel* like a better person when I'm with you. Marry me, *tesore mio*. Be my little princess for now and always.'

She threw her arms around his neck. 'Oh, Lucca, I can't believe this is happening. I love you *so* much. I've been distraught at the thought of you leaving but I didn't want to be one of those awfully clinging women who won't accept it when a fling is over.'

He looked down at her with a teasing smile. 'Hey, what is this? Are you calling our relationship a fling?'

Her eyes started to moisten again. 'Are we really engaged?'

'Sure are.'

She stalwartly blinked back tears. 'I'm not supposed to cry. It'll ruin my make-up and make me look like a panda. Madeleine will be furious if I—' She suddenly clapped her hands to her cheeks. 'Oh, my God! I have to get back to the cathedral! I left Adam with the bouquets. The photographer will be having kittens, puppies and ducklings by now.'

Lucca grabbed her hand. 'Come on. We'll take my car. It's waiting downstairs.'

A short while later Lottie burst out of the car, almost before they'd come to a halt. While she rushed inside, Lucca parked the car and, walking towards the church, pulled his phone from his pocket, dialling his brother's number, hoping that *this* time the time zones and planets would align and Orsino would answer. He understood his brother's need to get away by himself where no one could contact him but this special moment was something Lucca wanted to share with him before the rest of the world heard about it. 'Listen, you're probably halfway up a mountain, or rescuing puppies or something, but we need to talk. Gene and Giatrakos are playing games with us, but you probably already know that. I have some news. And no it's not a joke. It's the real deal. I wanted you to know first. Call me.'

Lottie floated down the aisle behind the bride and groom a short time later. Lucca and she had agreed on the race back to the church that they wouldn't steal the limelight by announcing their engagement until the bride and groom had left the reception. The knowledge of his love for her filled her with such happiness she was sure she was going to burst.

He loved her! He loved her! He loved her!

Lottie wanted to skip and jump and do a happy dance instead of walking down the aisle with such sedate pageantry. Her hands shook with excitement, making the bouquet quiver so much some petals fell off. At this rate there would be nothing left but the florist's wire by the time she got to the back of the church.

Yep. She was *definitely* going to burst. It would be *hours* before she could tell anyone. How would she stand it? She would have to tell someone. She would have to! Otherwise she would think she had dreamt it all.

Was Lucca finding it equally difficult? As she got a little closer she saw him standing at the back of the church, leaning against one of the pillars looking distinctly bored. He yawned widely and reached for his phone and started scrolling through his messages.

A worrying thought slipped under the guard of her newfound happiness. What if he'd been joking? What if this was all a setup? Another one of his puerile little jokes? A game he was playing?

Did he *really* love her?

Oh, God, what if he was only pretending so he could get his money?

What if in three days' time he left the island without her?

But as she walked past, Lucca looked up from his phone and gave her a secret message with his glinting dark eyes that was as loud and clear as if he had bellowed it from the bell tower: *I love you.*

* * * * *

If you enjoyed this book, look out for
the next instalment of
THE CHATSFIELD:
SOCIALITE'S GAMBLE
by Michelle Conder.
Coming next month.

THE CHATSFIELD

UNCOVERED!

Read on for an exclusive interview with Melanie Milburne

Creating a world as large as The Chatsfield must be very exciting—did you discuss the hotels with the other authors?

We had a great time discussing rooms, layouts, cocktails and even smells! Aromatic oils and body lotions and soaps exclusive to the hotel. In fact, we had so much fun discussing stuff we had to remind ourselves to get on and write the books!

What was the most fun bit about creating this luxurious, scandalous world?

The Chatsfield hotel world is top-end luxury, so it was great fun indulging in the fantasy of living the high life. After all, that's what the Modern™ series is all about.

Did you do any extra-special research for writing this book? A sneaky cocktail at an exclusive hotel perhaps?

Of course! It's a tough gig, but someone's got to do it. I'm always willing to make sacrifices for the sake of my art!

What did you most love about writing your story?

I loved Lucca because he was such a bad boy. He was so unapologetic for it and relished in shocking people whenever and wherever he could. I am such a Goody Two-Shoes, so I had to channel my evil twin to get into his character. So much fun!

When writing your hero and heroine's story, did they surprise you in any way?

The first thing that surprised me when I read the outline of my story was that I felt Charlotte didn't want to be called by her full name. She insisted on close friends and family calling her Lottie. I really felt she was speaking to me right from the start. Lucca was leaping off the page as soon as I put my fingers to the keyboard. I had to put my skates on to keep up with him!

To your mind, who is the most scandalous Chatsfield?

Definitely Lucca. Even though he is happily settled with Lottie, he will still continue to shock and stir. The only difference now is he won't let anything or anyone hurt Lottie.

If you could have given your hero or heroine a piece of advice before they started on their journey in your story, what would it have been?

For Lottie I would have said: *You are perfect as you are, you're not second-best or the spare part no one wants.*

For Lucca: *You don't have to hide your talents*

behind that brash façade. Show your sensitivity to the world. Don't be ashamed of it.

Name five things on your desk when you write.

A cup of tea.

A make-up brush that I use to brush cookie crumbs off my keyboard. (I know, I know. I shouldn't eat at the computer, but writing makes me hungry!)

A sheet of paper with notes on my characters as well as chapter numbers and pages.

Flowers of some sort.

My mobile phone, which I try to ignore when I'm writing, as Facebook and Twitter can be very time-consuming.

Do you listen to music when you write?

Sometimes I do, especially if someone else is in the house, as I can find it distracting. I love classical music, in particular Mozart or Beethoven, but I never listen to anything with lyrics while I'm writing (other than choral music in Italian or Latin) so I don't get pulled out of my story by singing along!

What is your worst habit when writing?

I'm quite possibly the most restless writer on the planet. I write a few sentences and then go downstairs for a cup of tea, bring it back up, drink half of it while I tap away and then I head off to the bathroom next to my office to check on my eyebrows or put on some lipstick, fuss with my hair—including the ones I keep finding on my chin—argh! Then I go back and write a bit more until I finally get on a roll and write for a couple of hours with numerous trips downstairs for more tea. Crazy, I know, but it works for me.

Do you have a writing routine? If so, could you share a bit about it with us?

I'm a morning person, but I hardly ever write in the morning. I do all the other stuff first. I get my e-mails sorted and anything businesslike out of the way. A quick trip to Facebook and Twitter and then I'm off for a swim and walking my dogs. All of this activity is my way of getting into the zone for writing. A lot of processing goes on that is deeply subconscious, so I let it all happen before I get in front of the computer so that my time there is productive. Looking at the bottom of the pool is much more inspiring than a blank screen. Trust me, it works!

UNDER THE MICROSCOPE

Read on for an exclusive interview with Lucca Chatsfield

If you had to pick your most public scandalous moment, what would it be?

Definitely the one that got me hauled into Christos's office. Being photographed wearing nothing but a leather codpiece is right up there when it comes to scandals. It was a good photo— one of my best angles in my opinion.

Was there an even more scandalous event that didn't make it into the press?

Nope. I made sure all my big ones got the attention they deserved. Although there was that one little moment I had a few years ago with that hot middle-aged housemaid back at my father's house…

What is your biggest secret?

I'm good at painting. It's not such a secret any more, but I'm cool with it.

What do you love most about Lottie?

Lottie is so darn cute when she purses up her lips and frowns at me in that schoolmarmish way. Gets me every time. She pretends she's cross with me, but I know how to make her laugh.

What were your first thoughts when you saw Lottie?

That she was uptight and buttoned-up but brooding with passion below the surface. I couldn't wait to press her buttons.

If your house were on fire and you could only save one thing, what would it be?

Lottie, but if she wasn't in danger, then my art portfolio. I have every drawing I've done since I was a kid.

What is the naughtiest thing you did at school?

I sprayed weedkiller on the school lawn in front of the headmaster's office. I won't tell you what it said. He never knew who did it. They didn't have CCTV back then.

What is your guiltiest pleasure?

I like a dry martini, shaken not stirred.

What is your worst habit?

I joke around when others expect me to be serious. I can't help it. I like to have fun.

What is your favourite film?

Anything by Quentin Tarantino. He's one cool but seriously twisted dude.

What present would you put beneath the Christmas tree for Lottie?

A miniature painting of her favourite place in the palace gardens where we kissed for the first time. I'm working on it as we speak. I want to surprise her with it. Don't tell!

How will you spend your first anniversary as a couple?

In bed making hot, smoking love. We want to have kids one day, but for now we want to enjoy each other. Besides, there are a couple more Kama Sutra positions we haven't nailed.

THE CHATSFIELD MR & MRS QUIZ

We get the real scoop on the inner workings of The Chatsfield's most notorious couple!!

What in your opinion is Lottie's best body part?

Lottie: Um, my hair?
Lucca: You want me to answer that truthfully or politely?

Do you have a nickname for Lottie and if so what?

Lottie: Angel cake
Lucca: Angel cake, because she's so good and so sweet.

What is Lottie's favourite alcoholic drink?

Lottie: I hardly ever used to drink but I love champagne cocktails now.
Lucca: Champagne cocktails, but don't let her have more than one. [Rolls eyes] Trust me. It's not worth it.

How many days have you been engaged for (at the time of the hen party)?

Lottie: 55
Lucca: I thought it was 45. [Shrugs and grins] Time flies when you're having fun.

What has been your favourite-ever holiday?

Lottie: [Sighs dreamily] When we went to Monte Carlo together.
Lucca: Monte Carlo, even though I was sick as a

dog for some of it.

What is Lottie's worst habit?

Lottie: I chew my nails, well, I used to. I'm growing them for the wedding.
Lucca: She picks at her cuticles.
Forfeit: Say the naughtiest word you know. Out loud.

Lucca, if you could dress Lottie for an evening on the town, what would you dress her in?

Lottie: [Blushes] He wouldn't dress me in anything.
Lucca: [Wicked grin] Cling film

What would you say is Lottie's favourite drink?

Lottie: Tea
Lucca: Tea in a fine bone china cup, not a mug

What one thing would Lucca save if the house were on fire (apart from Lottie)?

Lottie: His art portfolio
Lucca: My mobile phone with all my booty contacts on it. [Grins] Only kidding! My art portfolio.

If you could have a superhero power, what would you want?

Lottie: To make everyone in the world happy
Lucca: To make everyone happy and bring about world peace. Lottie would have made a great beauty-pageant contestant. She knows the drill. She makes me happy and I feel pretty chilled out when I'm with her.

What is Lucca's all-time favourite movie?

Lottie: [Reproachful frown] Anything with blood and guts and totally inappropriate humour in it.
Lucca: *Pulp Fiction* by Quentin Tarantino

What has been the most embarrassing thing Lottie's ever done?

Lottie: [Fiery blush] I'd rather not talk about it.
Lucca: The photo scandal when she was at finishing school, but she'd rather not talk about it. If you mention it again, I'll have to kill you.

What does Lottie think your most annoying habit is, Lucca?

Lottie: Making a joke out of everything, but really I love him for it.
Lucca: I never take things seriously, but I think she kind of likes that about me.

If Lottie were stuck on a desert island, what three things would she take?

Lottie: Lucca, of course, sunscreen and a towel
Lucca: Me. What else would she need?
Forfeit: Sing Happy Birthday backwards.

What is the most memorable day for you together since you met?

Lottie: The day of my sister's wedding when he asked me to marry him
Lucca: Her sister's wedding day. She didn't believe me when I told her I loved her. I should have been offended, but I guess she thought I was joking.

CHATSFIELD BAD BOY CAUGHT WITH TROUSERS DOWN!

Lucca Chatsfield has brought new shame and disgrace on The Chatsfield brand after images of him lying handcuffed to a bed in the London Chatsfield hotel wearing nothing but a black leather studded codpiece went viral.

Neither Lucca, nor his father, Gene, was available for comment, but a spokesperson for the high-end hotel chain, newly appointed CEO Christos Giatrakou, issued a brief statement to the press informing the public that the matter of Lucca's indiscretion had been dealt with internally and there would be no further comment.

From: Christos.Giatrakou@chatsfield.co.uk
To: Lucca.Chatsfield@chatsfield.co.uk
Subject: Meeting at 10 am.

Dear Lucca,

Unless you are in my office by 10 am today, you are without a trust fund. Got it?

C. Giatrakou

To: Christos.Giatrakou@chatsfield.co.uk
From: Lucca.Chatsfield@chatsfield.co.uk
Subject: Meeting at 10 am.

Cool it, dude, it was just a photo. No big deal. You should've seen the ones with the whip and the chains. WTG!

Cheers,

Lucca

PS Can we make it 11 am?

To: Lucca.Chatsfield@chatsfield.co.uk
From: Christos.Giatrakou@chatsfield.co.uk
Cc: Gene.Chatsfield.co.uk
Subject: Meeting at 10 am.

10 am. Sharp. No show. No trust fund.

CG

Lottie: R U CRZ?

Madeleine: Lol! He's a QT. Enjoy!

Lottie: Not ☺
Wot r u up to?

Madeleine: It's only 4 a month ICRWorse.

Lottie: UGTBKidding!

Madeleine: Ur rep is safe. U r not his type.

Lottie: Y?

Madeleine: U no

Lottie: IGTKillU!

Madeleine: TLK2UL8R Mwah!

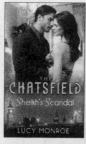

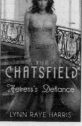

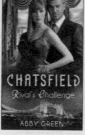

THE
CHATSFIELD®

Enter the intriguing online world of
The Chatsfield and discover secret
stories behind closed doors...

www.thechatsfield.com

Check in online now for your exclusive
welcome pack!

From: Lucilla.Chatsfield@thechatsfield.com

Sent: Tuesday, 6th May 2014 11:17 a.m.

To: Jessie.Loe@thechatsfield.com

Subject: Prince Sayid's arrival

Jessie,

Please check everything is in order for the arrival of Prince Sayid and his party.

And did Mr Brightman receive his complimentary hamper?

Please ensure everything is in order.

Thank you for staying late last night.

Lucilla

Did the hamper get delivered?
And why did Jessie need to stay late?
Discover Jessie's story, and much more,
at **www.thechatsfield.com**

@brightman_adam

So I'm being kicked out of #TheChatsfield Presidential Suite for 2 weeks. Don't they know who I am?? I blame @jessieloedown...

To follow this Presidential Suite scandal,
follow Adam Brightman
on Twitter **@brightman_adam**
or visit **www.thechatsfield.com**
to discover the whole story!